"I'm not sure I unders

"It's quite simple," he said, leaning back in his chair and surveying her with hooded eyes. "I find you very attractive."

His bluntness shocked and stirred her in equal measure. Beneath the lowered lids she discerned a glitter of desire.

An involuntary shiver—part fear, part keen anticipation—tightened her skin and paralysed her thoughts.

Kain examined her face, his cold eyes piercing and far too astute.

"I think the best way to deal with the situation is for you and me to become lovers."

"What?"

He bent his head and kissed her startled mouth. It was a claim, open and demanding, and it smashed through her barriers with shaming ease. She had no chance to think, no time to do anything but surrender to a compelling hunger that battered down her instinctive resistance.

"That's not fake," he said, his voice rough. "Admit it, Sable—you want me every bit as much as I want you."

With Valentine's Day coming up, it's the perfect opportunity to indulge in some romance, and where better than with eight new fantastic Harlequin Presents® stories!

This month we have bestselling author Lynne Graham with the second book in her PREGNANT BRIDES trilogy, *Ruthless Magnate, Convenient Wife*. Get whisked away to the stunning Moscow where ruthless billionaire Sergei Antonovich will stop at nothing to make the shy and virginal Alissa his convenient wife!

And please help us celebrate Carole Mortimer's 150th book, *The Infamous Italian's Secret Baby*. When one night leads to one baby, Bella Scott finds herself at the mercy of infamous Gabriel Danti!

Why not treat yourself with a wonderful story of blackmail in Robyn Donald's *The Rich Man's Blackmailed Mistress*. And Talos Xenakis's plans for revenge change when he discovers his mistress is pregnant in Jennie Lucas's *Bought: The Greek's Baby*.

Out this month is our first book in the BRIDE ON APPROVAL miniseries. Whether bought, sold, bargained for or bartered, these brides have no choice but to say I do. Be sure not to miss Caitlin Crews's debut book, *Pure Princess, Bartered Bride*.

Who will reunite the two Stefani diamonds, and become ruler? Find out in the last installment of THE ROYAL HOUSE OF KAREDES, *The Desert King's Housekeeper Bride* by Carol Marinelli. But the saga continues in April with DARK-HEARTED DESERT MEN. Four brooding sheikhs with a hint of Karedes in them.

And last, but by no means least, don't forget about any of our fabulous new miniseries coming out in 2010. The glamour, the excitement, the intensity just keep getting better.

Wow! 2010—this truly is the year of Presents! *Your everyday luxury*.

Robyn Donald

THE RICH MAN'S
BLACKMAILED MISTRESS

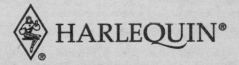

TORONTO • NEW YORK • LONDON
AMSTERDAM • PARIS • SYDNEY • HAMBURG
STOCKHOLM • ATHENS • TOKYO • MILAN • MADRID
PRAGUE • WARSAW • BUDAPEST • AUCKLAND

Recycling programs
for this product may
not exist in your area.

ISBN-13: 978-0-373-12896-9

THE RICH MAN'S BLACKMAILED MISTRESS

First North American Publication 2010.

www.eHarlequin.com

Printed in U.S.A.

All about the author...
Robyn Donald

Greetings! I'm often asked what made me decide to be a writer of romances. Well, it wasn't so much a decision as an inevitable conclusion. Growing up in a family of readers helped; after anxious calls from neighbors driving our dusty country road, my mother tried to persuade me to wait until I got home before I started reading the current library book, but the lure of those pages was always too strong.

Shortly after I started school I started whispering stories in the dark to my two sisters. Although most of those tales bore a remarkable resemblance to whatever book I was immersed in, there were times when a new idea would pop into my brain. It was my first experience of the joy of creativity.

Growing up in New Zealand gave me a taste for romantic landscapes and exotic gardens. But it wasn't until I was in my mid-twenties that I read a Harlequin® romance novel and realized that the country I love came alive when populated by strong, tough men and spirited women.

By then I was married and a working mother, but into my busy life I crammed hours of writing; my family have always been hugely supportive, even the various dogs who have slept on my feet and demanded that I take them for walks at inconvenient times. I learned my craft in those busy years, and when I finally plucked up enough courage to send off a manuscript, it was accepted. The only thing I can compare that excitement to is the delight of bearing a child.

Since then it's been a roller-coaster ride of fun and hard work and wonderful letters from fans. I see my readers as intelligent women who insist on accurate backgrounds as well as an intriguing love story, so I spend time researching as well as writing.

CHAPTER ONE

KAIN GERARD looked at his aunt with affection and exasperation. 'Not again!'

She bridled. 'It's not Brent's fault! He's just—'

'An idiot when it comes to women,' Kain supplied more than a little tersely. 'He falls violently in lust with the most unsuitable female in sight, showers her with gifts, promises her undying love, then wakes up one morning and realises he has nothing in common with her. Worse than that, she knows nothing about computers, which means he can't even hold a conversation with her. So he dumps her and she goes off and wails tearfully—and lucratively—to the media.'

'He just gets carried away,' Brent's mother protested weakly. 'He doesn't know what he really needs.'

Kain's brows rose. 'He seems to know exactly what he needs,' he said in his driest voice. Big breasts, long legs and a wet-lipped simper—those were Brent's criteria. 'Temporarily, anyway. Why are you concerned this time?'

'Kain, you—of all people!—know perfectly well he's just had a very well-publicised payout on his internet firm—more than twenty million dollars.' Amanda Gerard hesitated, before saying in a rush, 'And she's not his usual type. To start off with she's older than he is, and she's not a model or a game show hostess or a beauty contest winner.'

Kain's black brows met in a frown. 'So you think she's after the money.'

'Brent has a reputation for rather foolish generosity,' his mother said unwillingly.

'What evidence have you got that she's a shark?'

Not for the first time Amanda Gerard decided it was positively *sinful* that as well has being brilliant and inordinately successful, Kain should look like something out of a fantasy—six foot three, shoulders big enough for a couple of women to cry on, and the sort of lean, potent vitality that stopped any woman's breath.

Most men would have been more than content with that. But Kain also had perfect features, a mouth to send shivers down even *her* spine, and grey eyes that were a stunning contrast to olive skin and sable hair.

Brent was good-looking, but not even a doting mother's bias would allow her to put him in Kain's class.

She thrust a photograph at her nephew. 'Look.'

She watched that sexy, sculpted mouth compress and his eyes narrow into ice chips as he scanned the image. Finally he looked up. 'She's definitely a change from Brent's usual inamoratas. Who is she?'

'Sable Jane Martin.'

'Sable?'

'Well, that's what she calls herself.' His aunt dismissed the pretentious name with a curled lip. 'She's at least five years older than Brent, and you'll notice she isn't hanging onto him or gazing worshipfully—or seductively—into his eyes,' Amanda pointed out, adding, 'And he speaks differently about her.'

'So what is the problem?' Kain was fond of the aunt who'd brought him up after his parents died, but he deplored her fierce, overprotective love for her only child.

He had no illusions about his cousin; Brent was spoilt. His open good looks—not to mention his assets—meant that most women succumbed to his laid-back approaches. Because he'd never had to work for a woman's notice he'd probably been intrigued by the cool, touch-me-not air of the one in the photograph.

A little impatiently he said, 'Perhaps this time he's found a normal woman—one he can actually have a conversation with.'

'Do you consider someone whose father was the town drunk *normal*?'

'That's hardly her fault.'

She grimaced. 'I know that, but you have to admit she probably has serious issues.'

'How do you know her father's an alcoholic?'

'He was—he's dead now. She comes from Hawkes Bay, from a little town quite close to Blossom McFarlane, so I rang Bloss and asked her if she knew the girl.'

Kain concealed a smile. His aunt's network of old school friends were affectionately known in the family as Amanda's mafia. 'And what did Blossom McFarlane tell you about her?'

His aunt gave him a suspicious glance. 'Bloss not only knew her, she'd felt sorry for her when she was growing up, even admired her for her loyalty to her deadbeat father. After he died she worked for an elderly solicitor for a few months, but there was some scandal.' His aunt hesitated, then said in a rush, 'Bloss said it was all very hush-hush, but she thought it involved stealing.'

Kain didn't like the sound of that. 'By Sable Martin?'

'Yes. Anyway, if she did steal anything she got off lightly. Nothing was ever done about it, but she left town under a cloud.'

Kain looked down at the woman standing beside Brent in the photograph, an enigmatic half-smile curling her lips. Unlike his cousin's previous girlfriends Sable Jane Martin didn't ooze sexuality, but Kain could see the attraction. That cool air was a challenge in itself; combine it with a sleekly elegant figure and a mouth that promised carnal delights galore, and Brent probably hadn't stood a chance.

Echoing his thoughts, Amanda said bitterly, 'Brent's already spent the best part of thirty thousand dollars on her.'

'A car?'

She paused, then made up her mind to tell him. 'A diamond ring.'

And that, Kain decided, he liked even less. 'Did he tell you that?'

'Of course he didn't. He must have bought it before he moved into that ridiculous penthouse, because the valuation documents came to my address.'

Mildly shocked, Kain asked, 'And you opened the letter?'

'I didn't even look at the address,' she told him indignantly. 'Well, not until after I picked myself up off the floor!'

Kain leaned back in his chair. 'So what do you want me to do?'

'I thought you could get someone from your security branch to look into this Sable person,' his aunt said, a little diffidently this time.

'My security men are paid to look after my business interests, not my personal ones.'

'I know, but in this case...' Her voice trailed away.

Kain gave her a sardonic smile. 'I'll get them to check. As an employer I can't approve of stealing.'

'And I thought you might make a play for her,' his aunt said in a rush.

'There's no one quite so ruthless as a devoted mother,' Kain said cynically. 'You must be seriously worried if you're prepared to sacrifice Brent's feelings as well as my time, my reputation, and his opinion of me.'

'Since when have you cared about what Brent thinks of you?' she shot back, flushing.

Actually, he valued his friendship with his cousin, but if this Sable Martin turned out to be a thief he was quite prepared to do what he could to protect Brent from any entanglement.

And if Kain had learned anything in his life it was that everything, even his aunt's affection, came with a price tag. 'I'll get back to you.'

She wasn't satisfied, but she knew when to stop pushing. Kain had given his word, and that meant it would be done. If there was anything at all suspicious in Sable Jane Martin's past, he'd soon know.

Narrowing his eyes, Kain looked over the heads of the crowd. Auckland's pre-Christmas racing carnival was in full swing; New Zealand's summer had swept into town, and, as well as the graceful thoroughbreds, elegant women in exquisite clothes were parading for an extremely attractive prize.

Kain's gaze homed in on the woman wearing a simple, superbly cut dress in soft dove-grey that contrasted with the pale purity of her skin and a black shimmer of hair beneath the frivolous hat. High heels emphasised long, glorious legs, and the silk clung to a narrow waist and curves that were alluring without being opulent. The only colour in the outfit was the true, vivid red of the lipstick that emphasised the woman's sultry mouth.

Definitely not Brent's usual type.

From just behind Kain a woman said, 'That's Maire Faris's entry. It's superb, but she won't win.'

'Too restrained,' her companion agreed. 'The judges always go for feathers and tulle and lots of overt glamour at these events. Who's the model?'

Kain didn't try to resist the temptation to eavesdrop. Although they were a few paces away from him the women's voices—sharpened by a little too much of the freely available champagne—reached him clearly.

'Mark Russell's secretary. You know, the Russell Charitable Foundation.'

'She looks far too decadent for such a worthy institution—well, *stuffy* is probably a better word for it.'

The woman was right; Sable Jane Martin certainly didn't look as though she spent her days dealing with the poor and needy of the world.

'Oh, well,' the other woman said with a gurgle of laughter, 'I suppose even such an upright, philanthropic citizen as Mark Russell likes something good to look at in the office.'

Indeed, Kain thought sardonically. Eyes narrowing, he scanned the face of the woman they were discussing. The demure outfit couldn't mask a subtle, exotic sensuality that made the other women on the dais fade into the background.

Kain's mouth thinned. Brent, he thought mordantly, you're in real trouble with this one.

His security check had come up with a very nasty scandal. Like most workplace scandals it had been covered up, but Sable Jane Martin had been in it right up to her very pretty neck.

Once a thief, always a thief…

And blackmail was the most despicable of thefts, especially in this case. A man had killed himself because of it.

Somebody had to chisel Sable Jane Martin out of his too-impressionable cousin's life before she got her greedy hands on his money and broke his heart.

Getting Brent out of the way had been reasonably easy; Kain had pulled strings to offer him the trip of a lifetime, crewing on a barquentine that was recreating a famous nineteenth century voyage of discovery. However, if things got brutal and basic, Kain knew his relationship with his cousin would take a battering.

Still, better a few months of tension between them than Brent being cheated of the money he'd earned over the past few years through damned hard work and the application of his intelligence.

'She looks up for anything,' the second woman remarked astutely. 'But with great discretion. Perfect mistress material.' Both women laughed. 'Is she attached?'

'Oh, yes, she's moved in with young Brent Gerard,' her companion said dryly.

Kain stiffened. This he hadn't known—it must have happened just before Brent left.

'Brent Gerard? One of the—oh, yes, I remember now, the kid who set up that internet company and has just sold it for gazillions to some big overseas corporation?'

To Kain's company, actually. He was beginning to think that he should have stayed well out of it—although Brent had been ready to move on to something new.

'Yes, that's the one—Kain Gerard's cousin.'

'An excellent move on her part, but why doesn't she aim higher? Kain's unattached, and he's worth billions, not a measly twenty or so million.'

Good thinking, Kain thought with distaste. He might

suggest it to Sable Jane Martin. But a faint tinge of colour heated his sweeping cheekbones at the woman's next words.

'Besides, he looks like a god.' Her voice dropped into a sexy purr. 'I *adore* men who tower over me, especially when they've got olive skin and dark hair and pale, pale eyes that bore right into your soul and suggest all sorts of wickedly exciting things.'

With a sly laugh the first speaker said, 'Well, for her I suppose it's a case of better the millionaire in the hand than the billionaire in the bush. For all his brains Brent is easy pickings; his cousin is an entirely different kettle of fish.'

Whatever she was going to say next was stopped by her companion, who said, 'Oh, look, there's Trina Porteous beckoning us over.'

Grimly, Kain watched Brent's new fling walk gracefully across the platform to take her place beside the other contestants competing for the best-dressed award.

The information his security men had dug up would make Miss Butter-wouldn't-melt-in-her-luscious-mouth feel very, very uncomfortable.

And he'd have no hesitation at all in using it.

Tiny hairs on the back of Sable's neck lifted in a primitive reaction to danger. Her hand tightened around the dove-grey bag and her stomach contracted in a fight-or-flee response that startled her. For a moment her smile faltered before she forced herself to breathe slowly and the world righted itself again.

Until she met an icy scrutiny across the crowd that sent her pulse shooting into warp speed. Kain Gerard—Brent's cousin. And he knew who she was. A chilly emptiness expanded beneath her ribs.

Applause from the crowd startled her until she realised

that the next contestant had stepped up onto the dais. Relieved, she joined the polite clapping.

But that level, intimidating gaze remained fixed on her. Her breath locked in her throat. Embarrassed at being singled out by Kain Gerard, she angled her chin upwards in automatic defiance. Brent's cousin could project silent intimidation until the sun went down, but she wouldn't allow him to frighten her.

But that cold gaze made her so uneasy she had to fight a growing tension until the last contestant came onto the stage, a lovely nineteen-year-old blonde who was bound to win the contest with her bright, summery, carefree look.

Sure enough she did, accepting her prize with a bubbly delight that reinforced the carnival atmosphere.

'Well, we gave it our best,' the elderly woman who'd designed Sable's costume told her when the crowd had filtered away to get good places for the last race, the big one of the day.

Sable smiled down at her. 'I'm sorry I didn't do your dress justice.'

'My dear, you wore it superbly. Here they want young and innocent and fresh, a salute to summer. You are sophisticated and stylish and a little bit mysterious—the sort of woman I'm designing for. I didn't expect to win, but even reaching the finals will be very good publicity for me.'

She turned her head as someone came up behind Sable. 'Hello, Kain,' she said, a note of surprise colouring her tone. 'I didn't realise you were back from wherever you've been these past months. I suppose you've got a horse running in the Cup?'

'I have.'

Deep and cool, his voice held a note of unsparing authority that sent little shivers through Sable. She stiffened her spine and tried to look calm and controlled.

'Is it going to win?' Maire asked.

'Of course,' he said with such calm confidence that Sable wondered if he'd managed to fix the race.

'What's its name? I'll go and put a bet on it before the tote closes.'

'Black Sultan.'

'Very appropriate,' Maire said dryly. 'Thanks so much.'

He said, 'You haven't introduced us, Maire.'

The older woman looked surprised. 'Oh—sorry, I assumed you two would know each other.'

Reluctantly, Sable turned.

Her dark eyes clashed with glacial grey ones. Bludgeoned by sensation, a bewildering mixture of apprehension and violent awareness, she dragged in a swift breath. She'd seen pictures of Brent's cousin, of course, and during the past few minutes she'd been uncomfortably aware of his coldly measuring gaze, but not even that had prepared her for the potent impact of his brand of male charisma.

'Sable, this is Kain Gerard,' her companion told her. 'I'm sure I don't have to tell you anything much about him—he turns up in the media quite often.'

'Not of my own volition,' he said crisply.

'No one could call you a publicity hound,' she conceded. 'Kain, meet Sable Martin, who should have won the prize up there.'

'Indeed she should.' Kain's tone produced an unfamiliar meltdown in Sable's spine. He took the hand she automatically extended, his fingers closing around hers. 'You were robbed.'

'I don't think so.' His touch set off strident alarms within her. And when she spoke her voice was pitched too low and sounded far too breathy...too *impressed*.

A little too hastily she added, 'The winner was just what they were looking for—a holiday spirit. And she wore her clothes very well.'

He said smoothly, 'Do you plan to watch the next race?'

Before Sable had a chance to come up with some excuse, her companion said, 'Of course we do, but first I'm going to put a bet on your horse.' Purposefully she started off towards the tote.

'You're not betting?' Kain Gerard commented when Sable made no attempt to follow her.

'No.'

He said, 'Let me stake you—barring accidents, my horse will win.'

'It's all right, thank you,' she said, warily conscious of the interested glances they were attracting. 'What about you? Don't you want to put some money on your horse?'

'I've already done that,' he told her, flashing her a killer smile that curled her toes inside the impractical, beautiful shoes she was wearing. 'Though as he's the favourite, he won't pay much.' Without altering his tone he said, 'You're a friend of my cousin's, I believe. Brent Gerard.'

'Yes,' she said neutrally.

Brent had told her all about his older cousin, inadvertently revealing that his open admiration of Kain had a thread of chagrin running through it.

Standing beside the man, every cell in her body humming, Sable could understand Brent's reaction; it would take a very secure young man to keep his confidence intact against such formidable competition.

Kain had been a billionaire before he reached thirty, Brent had told her enviously. 'His parents left him a controlling stake in one of New Zealand's most progressive companies as well as a hefty inheritance that gave him a damned good start on his quest for world domination.' Then he'd given her a charmingly rueful smile. 'But the real secret of his success is his drive and truly impressive brilliance, plus an uncanny knack for spotting trends.'

He'd paused, then finished significantly, 'And his ruthlessness. He's a bad man to cross.'

Wishing she'd gone with Maire, Sable pretended to examine the crowd. Instinct warned her that Brent had been right. Formidable determination was as much a part of Kain Gerard as his height and his broad shoulders and his arrogantly handsome face.

No wonder he was a hit with women. Brent hadn't been quite so open about that aspect of his cousin, but Sable had read some interesting gossip.

And now she believed it all. He was—well, *overwhelming* was about the only word that came to mind. And although he seemed pleasant enough, his glance held more cool assessment than admiration.

Feeling a chill, Sable glanced up to see if a cloud had swallowed the sun. No, the sky was as radiantly blue as it had been all day. She straightened her spine and matched Kain's assessing gaze.

He said, 'I gather you're a model?'

If Brent had talked at all about her, Kain must know perfectly well that she wasn't.

'Far from it,' she returned. 'Maire's established her new salon next to where I work, and when her model let her down she talked me into this because I'm almost the same size and colouring.' She gave him a carefully bland smile. 'As soon as she gets back we'll promenade around so more people can see the outfit.'

And then she was going. Apart from feeling absurdly conspicuous, her feet were killing her.

One black brow lifted, but all Kain said was, 'I'll stay until she returns.'

'There's no need,' she stated.

He smiled down at her. Deep within Sable something shattered into a million pieces, each one piercing her with excitement. Shocked, she managed a pale smile in return, then looked away, hugely grateful to see Maire on her way back to them.

Once she'd reached them Kain said, 'Why don't you both come and watch the race with me on the lawn?'

Bristling, Sable thought it wasn't so much a request as an order.

Her companion, however, beamed at him. 'I'm surprised you're not watching from the Presidential Club.'

He shrugged. 'We can go there if you want to, but I thought you'd want every chance to show off that pretty dress. There won't be any television cameras in the Club area.'

His gaze drifted down the dress, setting off alarms in every cell in Sable's body. Not that there was anything sensuous about that inspection; she'd been the target of lustful looks often enough to recognise its complete lack of desire.

Yet she felt harried, hunted, the object of some careful plan. Telling herself not to be so stupid, she accompanied them.

Once on the lawn, Sable understood Maire's rapid agreement. Everywhere she looked she met glances— some covert, some very open, but all intent on Kain Gerard and the two women he was escorting.

Although he nodded at people he knew, he didn't stop. When a waiter appeared he suggested, 'Champagne for you both?'

Maire accepted, but Sable said, 'No, thank you.'

'It's hot. You'll need something to cool you down,' he said, and gave the waiter an order for two glasses of champagne and one of the Cup special.

When Sable opened her mouth to tell him she didn't want anything alcoholic his lips curved again, and her heart flipped in her chest.

That smile was dangerous—and he knew its effect on women. He knew too much, she thought in rare confusion as her knees demanded she find a place to sit down.

He was too much—too much *everything*. Height always drew attention, but it wasn't just his height or his dominant features and a mouth hinting at vast expertise that turned her bones to water. Kain exuded an aura of compelling power that was both a reassurance and a threat.

'It's non-alcoholic,' he told her as the waiter returned with two flutes of champagne and a tall glass containing a concoction that looked deliciously refreshing. 'Peach and strawberry fizz.'

'Thank you,' she said stiffly, irritated to discover it tasted as good as it looked.

Someone came up and greeted Maire, who excused herself to engage in animated conversation. Niggled by uncomfortable tension, Sable looked down at the track as the horses started to file out to the starting gate.

'Which is yours?' she asked to fill in the silence.

'Number thirteen—the black,' he said, and pointed him out.

Another splendid beast, she thought ironically, so fit its muscles were almost bursting through the sleek midnight hide. 'Why are you so sure he'll win?'

'He's at his peak now, and he has the best form. There's

always the chance of a mishap, of course, but he should lead them home.'

He did, to wild cheers that proclaimed he was a favourite with the crowd as well as the punters. In spite of herself Sable was caught up in the moment, clapping excitedly and turning to Kain when it was over, her face alight. 'He's fantastic, isn't he? He just *blitzed* them! Where's he racing next?'

Her heart gave an unexpected lurch when he looked down at her, and the joyful tumult seemed to die away into silence.

She tried to lower her lashes, to look away, but that enigmatic grey gaze locked her into some kind of stasis.

Before he could answer he was enveloped by a mob of laughing, chattering friends as well as journalists with photographers in tow.

Intensely relieved, Sable stood back a little, envying him the formidable assurance with which he accepted handshakes from the men and kisses from a variety of women. She felt oddly alone, disconnected from the brightly dressed crowd and the laughter; the sun seemed breezy and uncomfortable, the crowd noise too loud, too shrill.

So? she thought, sipping some more of her drink. In every way that matters you've been alone all your life. And you gave up wallowing in self-pity the day you left Hawkes Bay for Auckland.

But it was just as well she wasn't likely to see much more of Kain Gerard.

Without looking at her he reached out and snagged her hand, drawing her to him as he said, 'Come with me. I'm going to congratulate the jockey and the trainer.'

Sable tugged uselessly. She said in a low, angry voice, 'I'm supposed to be showing off this dress.'

'If you're with Kain, you're going to be in every photograph,' Maire said brightly. 'Away you go.'

Sable's indignant glare clashed with coolly amused grey eyes. After a moment's hesitation she gave in, allowing herself to be escorted through the press of people until the flash from a camera startled her into flinching.

Kain's hand cupped her elbow more firmly. 'Throw them a smile,' he advised with an edge of cynicism in his deep voice. 'That's all you have to do—look elegant and confident. You can do that.'

Keeping her eyes fixed on the activity in the Birdcage, she forced a smile as she tossed off a reply. 'I'll have you know I have to suffer to get this elegant! These shoes are killers on the grass.' Shoe porn, Maire had called the grey sandals with their vertigo-inducing heels.

He glanced down. Something flickered in his hard eyes, but his voice was bland when he said, 'From a spectator's viewpoint, the sight of your feet in them is definitely worth the pain.'

Why did it seem this conversation was being conducted on two levels—one with words, the other with the subtle shift of tone and emphasis and the silent language of movement and gesture?

To her relief someone caught his attention and he turned away from her. Reluctantly Sable had to admire the way he dealt with the journalists and photographers—his charm not hiding an uncompromising authority.

Eventually he left her to lead the horse around the enclosure in a lap of honour. Sable watched them stride out with matching masculine grace, the sun striking blue highlights from the horse's glossy hide and from Kain's head.

'Two of a kind.' Half-envious, half-humorous, the trainer echoed her thoughts from beside her.

Sable took in a deep breath, calling on her surface gloss of sophistication. Until then she'd been stumbling along like any green girl, but now, with Kain's presence removed, she could regroup her forces.

'Does the horse have grey eyes?' she enquired, smiling to show she was joking.

He gave a snort of laughter. 'No, but he's a tough beast, and when he makes up his mind it's damned hard to change it. And he's honest; once he's committed, he throws his heart into every race.'

'What more could you want in a horse? Or a man?' she returned lightly. 'Isn't it a glorious day?'

Kain and the horse headed back as the trainer smiled at her. 'One of the best,' he agreed, stepping out to take the reins from Kain's lean hand.

Kain said, 'Right, let's go.'

They started to leave, only to have a photographer call, 'One more, Kain.'

He turned his head and said coolly, 'Of course,' and before Sable could move out of range he scooped her against his lean body and held her, smiling down into her startled eyes and saying, 'This one's for the social pages. Relax and think of the publicity for Maire.'

Far too conscious of his strength against her, she felt herself stiffen. The chatter of the crowd dulled; inwardly cringing, she sensed avid eyes on them both.

'Smile,' he commanded quietly, the handsome face amused.

Her brows lifted. 'Why?'

'Because if you don't everyone who sees this is going to think you're besotted.' And when she responded with a haughty glare he bent his head to say even more softly, 'Perhaps I should kiss you.'

CHAPTER TWO

'DON'T you dare,' Sable hissed, but some wild emotion leapt into shocking life inside her. Kain's arctic eyes narrowed, and she froze, her heart hammering.

The photographer's voice jarred her back into reality. 'Hey, that's great! Thank you.'

The moment Kain's arm relaxed Sable twisted away. Summoning a smile took all of her concentration, but there was no way to hide the lingering heat that burned her cheeks.

What the *hell* did Kain Gerard think he was playing at?

And why did he cause such novel turmoil inside her?

'Maire should be pleased with that,' he said with no visible sign of emotion.

Sable suppressed the urge to say that for someone who'd denied seeking publicity he'd almost courted it for the older woman. Instead she murmured, 'You're very kind to her.'

His mouth twisted. 'She was a friend of my mother's and I admire her entrepreneurial spirit.'

Well, she knew only too well how strong and tight the circle of influential people could be.

Maire came up, her slightly perplexed gaze going from

one face to the other. 'Thank you, Kain,' she said swiftly. 'You've been great. Are you ready to leave, Sable?'

'Yes.' Sable kept her voice level, hoping neither realised she felt as though she'd just been thrown a lifeline. Without letting her smile reach her eyes, she turned to Kain and said formally, 'Thank you for an interesting experience.'

'My pleasure entirely.'

His smooth, amused voice infuriated her.

Kain watched her walk gracefully away, only a certain rigidity to her slender body indicating that she was angry. She was looking down at the woman beside her with what seemed genuine interest.

Nice going, he thought, although threatening to kiss her in front of thousands of people and a media audience might not have been a good move.

But it had been worth it for that moment when she'd let her guard slip and he'd seen the heat kindle in her dark eyes. Like it or not—and he suspected she didn't—she was very definitely aware of him.

So things were going his way. And he was, he thought with cold, controlled satisfaction, a much tougher challenge than Brent.

After changing into her own clothes, Sable refused Maire's offer of a lift and walked off to catch a bus, her feet in their flat sandals fervently thanking her with each step. Smiling at the thought, she promised them that when she got home she'd soak them in something warm and soothing.

'I think I like this look even more,' Kain Gerard said from behind her.

She froze, her heart rate increasing madly. He smiled lazily down, but his grey eyes were hooded against the sun, and the smile held something she distrusted.

He commented, 'Very cool, very...innocent.'

The cynical intonation to the last word made her angry. White happened to suit her and the dress was a favourite of hers. 'That's long out of date,' she said, infusing the words with a faint scorn.

'The dress?' He swung into place beside her.

Sable thought seriously of telling him she didn't want his company, only to give a mental shrug. The bus queue was no place for billionaires; he'd leave soon enough.

She replied, 'The connection of white with chastity.'

Kain gave her an amused glance. Furious with herself, Sable pretended to examine a large purple car that was proceeding with stately dignity down the road. Stupid! Why hadn't she just ignored his provocative remark?

Because he unnerved her so much it scrambled her brain, that's why.

Kain said thoughtfully, 'Perhaps I am old-fashioned.'

Her glance probably told him more than she wanted it to, for he sent her a bland smile.

'That sounds rather sweet,' she said kindly, then nodded in the direction of the buses. 'I'm going this way, so goodbye.'

'Aren't you using Brent's car?'

She felt a tightness in her chest. 'No,' she said shortly.

It had been a mistake to move into Brent's apartment. But his offer of a place to stay while she found a new home had seemed a lifesaver. However, it hadn't taken her long to realise he'd seen it as a step forwards in a relationship she'd been at pains to keep at a friendly level.

So she had to find new lodgings by the time he got back from his unexpected holiday.

Kain's voice broke into her thoughts. 'I'll give you a lift back.'

Turning her face away from his too-keen scrutiny, she

shook her head firmly. 'No, thank you,' she said, and strode towards the waiting bus.

Kain watched the sun gleam across the ebony satin of her hair, its sleek chignon setting off her fine features and that wanton mouth, now firmly under control.

Playing it cool. Well, he'd expected that; she'd be stupid to ditch one prospect until she had the next one—the richer one—hooked and reeled in. A humourless smile curved his mouth as he walked towards the members' car park. He knew how this game went, and he'd enjoy playing it for a while.

'Sable, *who* is *that*? Oh—my—God, he's *faaaabulous*.'

'Hang on,' Sable said absently without taking her eyes from the computer screen. The boss's daughter habitually spoke in italics, and fell in love with a new man every couple of days.

'He's coming here!'

'Well, this *is* the reception area.'

Poppy's voice dropped to a low whisper. 'Oh, oh, *oh*, I know who he is.'

'Hush, he might hear y—' The word dried on her tongue when she looked up and saw Kain Gerard strolling towards her, breathtakingly masculine in a formal city suit.

Literally breathtaking; she had to force her lungs to drag in some air, and beneath her ribs her heart set up a wayward rhythm that echoed in her ears.

'Sable,' he said with a devastating half-smile. 'How are you?'

Hearing Poppy take a swift indrawn breath, Sable hastily said, 'Hello, Kain. Can I help you?'

'You can show me the pictures that will be sold in the charity auction.'

The Russell Foundation held an annual art auction, and

because one day she planned to work as an events manager, Sable always volunteered her services to organise the evening. This year it was to be held in the ballroom of a huge modern mansion, the perfect place to show off the avant-garde pictures and sculptures now waiting in the Foundation's warehouse.

Her first impulse was to hand Kain over to Poppy, but the slight emphasis on the first word of his answer made her hesitate and look up at him. The moment her eyes met his warning gaze she realised he understood what she intended to do—and was warning her against it.

Poppy was young and untried enough to be hurt by rejection. And although the paintings and sculpture weren't yet officially on exhibition, Kain Gerard knew—as Sable did—that no one would refuse to show them to him.

Money talks, she thought, unable to show her chagrin, and big money talks big.

Evenly, her voice aloof, Sable replied, 'Yes, of course.'

Heart skipping into an uneven rhythm, she closed the computer and straightened up to walk towards him, glad that she'd worn a dress in the bold, clear red that gave colour to her pale skin and made her eyes dark and deep and—she hoped—impossible to read.

She was fiercely aware of Kain on a level so basic she had no command over it. Every cell seemed to recognise him, as though his touch had imprinted her for life.

And that ridiculous overreaction scared her.

'Come this way,' she said in her most modulated voice, hoping that he hadn't noticed her tension.

Silently he surveyed the exhibition with an impassive face. This year the committee that oversaw the choice of artists had chosen those with postmodern credentials, and because the exhibition and auction gave them excellent publicity most had really let themselves go.

Sable kept her features controlled. Somehow, she didn't think Kain would be impressed—unless he was buying an investment. You didn't have to like investments.

He surprised her by asking, 'What do you think of them?'

'My opinion isn't worth anything,' she evaded.

'You don't like them.'

How had he noticed that? Uneasily she said, 'I don't know anything about this sort of art so my personal opinion means nothing. I can get an expert to discuss them with—'

He stopped her with a glance and a single word. 'No.'

For the next half hour he strolled along the row of pictures, standing back occasionally to get a better view, looking more closely at others. Sable wondered just what was going on behind that handsome face.

Finally he said, 'Tell me what you really think.'

Exasperated by his persistence, she returned shortly, 'The only useful comments I could make would just be parroting what I've heard.'

'I don't want that—I want your opinion. You must have some idea—wasn't your father an artist? Angus Martin? The Art Gallery has several of his pictures and one stunning watercolour.'

Touched—and made extremely cautious by the fact that he'd heard of her father—she said, 'If you've seen it you'd know that he didn't paint like this.'

'But you must have heard him discuss art.'

Oh, yes, endless discussions that had degenerated into maudlin regrets that his skills no longer matched his vision, that he'd drunk away whatever talent he'd once had...

Faced with a determination that matched her own—

and because Kain Gerard might be prepared to spend a lot of money on this very good cause—she said reluctantly, 'I don't understand the artists' visions or their objectives, and I don't know enough about art to relate to their techniques.'

'Why does that annoy you?'

You annoy me, she thought, irritated with him and with herself for being so affected by him.

Shrugging, she returned lightly, 'Because I feel as though I'm missing out on something—on some secret that others understand.'

He pinned her with a considering stare that lasted two seconds too long, then nodded. 'Fair enough. Did you see our photograph in the newspaper?'

She'd very carefully avoided looking at the social pages. 'No, I didn't.'

His smile told her he didn't believe her. 'A pity. I'm afraid it won't garner Maire Faris good publicity—the dress doesn't show to advantage. However, her name is mentioned.'

Something in his tone made her uncomfortable. She said stiffly, 'I'm glad.'

Fixing his gaze on a canvas that to Sable looked like a too-dramatic representation of a bad headache, he asked with casual interest, 'Have you heard from Brent lately?'

'No.' She stole a glance at his profile, strong and commanding. Something very strange happened to her stomach—no, her heart.

Ignore it, she told herself sturdily, and said with brittle composure, 'Apparently he's not going to be able to contact anyone for a month or so. Rather ironic that a man whose life is focused on the internet should deliberately leave himself without access to it.'

'I think he's ready to go cold turkey for a while,' Kain said. He delivered a low-wattage version of that killer smile. 'Thank you for showing me around.'

She said formally, 'I hope we'll see you at the auction.' He'd been invited; she'd have to check to see if he'd accepted.

'Possibly.'

Her complete ignorance had probably blown any chance of a good sale, she thought with wry resignation and accompanied him back to the reception area.

Poppy looked up, her pretty face awed. With some surprise Sable noted the smile he bestowed on the younger girl. Friendly, appreciative, it showed none of the antagonism that seemed to underlie his attitude to her.

In response, Poppy blushed brilliantly, melting without any visible sign of resistance.

Afterwards Sable had to endure the younger woman's sighing comments, relieved when lunchtime came—only to find herself being warned during the meal by Maire.

'Kain's nothing like his cousin,' the older woman said, eyeing the huge muffin she'd chosen. 'Brent's a nice boy—bright too, and he obviously has a good business brain when it comes to the internet—but he doesn't have Kain's charisma.'

'No,' Sable agreed, touched in some secret part. She'd been on her own since she was seventeen, and the only womanly influence in her life had been her father's neighbour Miss Popham, an elderly woman whose brisk, practical attitude hadn't encouraged confidences.

Don't go there, she thought and hurriedly transferred her attention back to Maire. 'Don't worry, I'm not going to fall for either of them.'

'It's not always that easy,' the designer said shrewdly, 'especially as you're living with Brent.'

'I'm not—I'm staying in his apartment until I find a suitable flat.' Because it was important, she emphasised, 'We aren't lovers—or even possible lovers.'

Maire lifted incredulous brows.

Harried, Sable expanded, 'He's years younger than me, for heaven's sake, and I feel positively ancient when I'm with him. We haven't got that sort of relationship—haven't even exchanged so much as a kiss!'

'But he wants to,' Maire said pragmatically.

Sable sighed. 'It's not going to happen. He knows that now.'

'So why did you move in with him?'

Normally she wouldn't have considered it, but one weekend while Sable was away her flatmate had held a party, a wild affair that had led to a wholesale trashing of the villa they shared.

Briefly she explained, and Maire tut-tutted. 'Your name was on the lease, was it?'

'Yes.' It hadn't surprised Sable when she and her repentant flatmate had been asked to leave, but she'd been horrified to discover that her landlady—an elderly widow—had let the insurance lapse.

Because, she'd informed Sable, she'd considered her to be a responsible person who'd look after the place. And perhaps because she'd just forgotten. Legally, of course, Sable wasn't obliged to pay for the damage, but for her own peace of mind she needed to. The landlady had been kind to her, and she hated to leave with a stain on her conscience—already stained enough, she thought grimly. Repayment had emptied out her bank account and left her feeling intensely vulnerable.

Firmly changing the subject, she said, 'As for Kain, he's not the sort of man I'm comfortable with.' She paused, then added with some irony, 'I find him too over-whelming.'

'You must be the only woman in New Zealand to feel that way.' Maire sighed and slathered some butter on her muffin. 'All right, I've had my say. If I remember anything of my far-distant youth, it's how unwelcome advice can be.'

'I didn't mean to sound abrupt—'

Maire laughed. 'You didn't. I was just being meddle-some. I've known Kain since he was a kid and even then he was the most self-sufficient person I've ever come across. Just as well—he was only twelve when his parents were killed, and at eighteen he took over the family business because it was going under. He had to grow up really fast.'

Interested in spite of herself, Sable said, 'He and Brent don't seem to have anything in common.'

'Pretty much nothing beyond brains and genes.' She sighed. 'I really, *really* wanted to get my hands on the woman young Brent was with last year. She had a great body and she was good-looking, but if she'd come to me I'd have steered her away from cleavage and clothes so tight you could see the pores of her skin under the fabric. Not that Brent seemed to mind,' she said wryly, adding, 'Kain, on the other hand, goes for class and intelligence and sophistication in his lovers.'

'So who's the present incumbent?' Sable tried to make her voice only mildly interested.

'Oh, he hasn't *lived* with any of them.' Maire shot her an amused glance. 'And even though he must be ten or so years older than his cousin, he's probably had fewer lovers than Brent. Their attitudes differ; Brent treats women like buying from a chain store, whereas Kain chooses a more select wardrobe from a designer.'

But he knew infinitely more about women than Brent, Sable thought, an inward shiver tightening her skin.

She stopped herself from asking more questions because she most emphatically was *not* interested in Kain Gerard's love life.

'Of course there was a six-month period when he and that film star—Jacie Dixon—were a very hot item. They kept it discreet and low-key, but the photos in the tabloids just about smoked off the pages.'

Sable hoped that her amused smile hid an ignoble pang of something that most emphatically was *not* envy. 'I wouldn't have picked you for a keen follower of the tabloids.'

'I'm not, but my granddaughter is obsessed with celebrities.' Her companion sighed again. 'I know far more about the secret lives of Hollywood stars than I care to, believe me. Fiona's a sucker for a good-looking man, and she has a secret stash of photos of Kain Gerard.'

'Well, she's got taste,' Sable said lightly. 'How old is she?'

'Fourteen. Why?'

'Because that sort of thing usually passes by the time they hit sixteen. It will be pop stars then.'

Maire gave her look, part horror, part resignation. 'I hope not. At least Kain's a good role model—no drugs, no run-ins with the cops, no drunken outings splashed across the newspapers, and a decent discretion in his affairs.'

Sable changed the subject, but later that night she wondered why Maire had felt it necessary to bring up the subject of Kain Gerard.

Surely she hadn't discerned the surprising sensations he roused in Sable, that sharp, powerfully—and *entirely*—physical response that brought a rush of adrenaline to heighten her every sense?

Possibly; Maire was astute and one of the reasons she was a good designer was her instinctive understanding of people.

Grimacing, Sable put Kain Gerard out of her mind.

Later that week she dressed for the first display of the art, a warehouse affair to show appreciation for the artists, the committee who'd worked so hard, and the various patrons of the Foundation, not to mention the organisations that would benefit from the auction. The following morning the pictures would be transferred to the Browns' mansion.

Mentally going over her list to make sure she'd left nothing undone, Sable slid into a pair of black trousers bought from a second-hand shop specialising in designer cast-offs. It was two years since they'd been a fashion item, but the cut was timeless and they fitted her perfectly.

No more clothes until she'd paid off the debt she owed to her landlady, she thought, getting into a collarless red shirt cut so that it hugged her body. Tiny silver buttons arrowed from her throat to her waist. The mock-coral arm cuff and her high-heeled boots repeated the colour of the shirt and her lipstick.

'Too much of a muchness?' she wondered, staring at her reflection.

Then she shrugged. What did she care? As she'd be on duty she didn't want to look overdressed, but she certainly didn't need to fade into the background either.

Poppy and her mother were checking the arrangements when she walked in. The younger woman came racing across.

'You look terrific!' she gushed, eyes darting to take everything in. 'I really, really like the way you put your hair up—how does it stay so burnished and silky looking?'

'Willpower.' Sable grinned at her. 'That's a super dress. Love the necklace.'

Poppy grimaced. 'Thanks, but I'd give anything to look as glam as you. I'm like Mum—doomed to prettiness.'

Laughing, Sable shook her head at her. 'Millions of women and girls long for a similar fate.'

'I'd give *anything* for style,' Poppy said earnestly.

Her mother came over, gave Sable an assessing look that smoothed into approval and said, 'Everything seems to be under control, Sable. Is there anything I can do to help?'

'Just keep an eye on everyone and let me know if you see any problems.'

The older woman frowned, then hastily relaxed her face. 'Mark's afraid some of the artists might drink too much and start arguing. Remember the barney that erupted last year?'

Sable shrugged. 'I'll be alert, but it's a help to have someone ready to move in on any argument that looks as though it might get out of hand. If you could keep an eye on anything that might erupt I'd be grateful. I find that introducing someone else—especially someone who looks as though they might be a buyer—usually stops people getting too passionate. It should be fine.'

It was. Everyone behaved themselves, the rich and the social made appropriate noises when confronted by the pictures they'd theoretically come to see, and as the evening was winding down a famous rugby front-row player, a figurehead for a prominent charity, astounded everyone by expounding with insight and appreciation on the use of symbolism in one of the more outrageous pictures.

'Learning anything?' a deep, dark voice said from behind Sable.

The tiny hairs on the back of her neck standing up

straight, Sable drew in a quick breath and composed her expression. Only then did she turn her head to meet Kain Gerard's darkly hooded eyes. In the stark black-and-white elegance of evening clothes he looked—utterly *gorgeous*...

How, in those supremely civilised clothes, tailored for him by a genius, did he also manage to emit a hard-edged aura of danger?

Her dancing heartbeat shocked her, but she met the cool challenge of his survey with slightly raised brows as she answered, 'Somewhat to my surprise, yes.'

'Guilty of stereotyping, Sable?' He stretched her name, lengthening it into a lazy drawl that came close to a caress. Or a taunt...

Whatever, it did amazing things to her body, summoning a wildfire heat. 'I'm afraid so,' she said crisply. 'In future I'll remember that rugby players can be intelligent as well as athletic.'

'Why Sable?' When she stared at him he elaborated smoothly, 'It's an unusual name.'

'When I was born I had a cap of black hair about the same length and texture as my father's brushes. He decided to call me Sable.' She noticed his empty hands and seized an opportunity to regroup her defences. 'Let me get you a drink and something to eat.'

Kain looked around the room; within seconds a waiter materialised with a salver of champagne, followed immediately by another carrying a tray of delicious titbits.

Made even crosser by this indication of Kain's innate presence, Sable decided to assert herself. 'Do have some champagne. And if you like mushrooms, I can heartily recommend those stuffed ones.'

He said, 'Thank you,' and managed the acceptance of

glass and mushroom with deftness. 'How about you? Your glass is almost empty.'

Her father's addiction had made Sable wary; she rarely drank more than one glass of wine. With a quick smile she said to the waiter, 'Nothing, thank you.'

But the wretched man glanced at Kain, waiting for his short nod before moving away. Amused but resigned, she accepted that any good waiter would recognise an alpha male when he saw one!

And Kain was certainly a number one alpha.

'How nice that you came,' she said brightly. 'Have you spoken to Mark—Mark Russell?'

'I came to see you.'

Startled, she looked up. Although a smile curved that sculpted mouth, his pale eyes were burnished and unreadable. 'Why?' she asked bluntly.

'Do you want it spelt out?' he asked softly, his narrowed eyes holding hers.

Heat flared in the pit of her stomach when he finished, 'Not here, I think. How much longer before you can get away?'

Many of the guests had already left, but quite a few were still busily networking. Excitement pulsing hotly through her, Sable tried and failed to catch Mark's eye. 'I don't— not until everyone's left.'

She sounded like a wimp, she thought despairingly, not a sophisticated woman who knew how to deal with men of his sort.

Except that she'd never come across another man with Kain's particular combination of powerful personality and spectacular good looks.

'I'm sure we can arrange something.' Coolly he took her elbow and she found herself being shepherded across the room to where Mark stood talking to one of the artists.

'Hey,' she said, shaking off her unnatural obedience. 'What are you doing?'

'Saying thank you and goodbye.' Kain's voice was implacable, but he gave her a narrow smile that somehow invited complicity. 'I have excellent manners,' he told her serenely.

Amusement bubbled up. 'Oh, really?' she parried, adding on a challenging note, 'Dragging women around by the arm isn't polite in any etiquette book I've ever read.'

He grinned. Her stomach lurched, and to her chagrin she felt tingles of sensation scud down her spine, ending up as smouldering heat in the pit of her stomach.

'Sometimes brute force is the only way to get what you want,' he said, and nodded at Mark Russell.

Mark had already seen them coming towards him, his smile broadening when he recognised Kain.

What followed was a comedy, Sable thought, one in which she didn't know her part.

Kain said easily, 'Hello, Mark. I'm just about to snaffle Sable.'

Was that what he'd meant when he referred to brute force? It was about as subtle as a sledgehammer!

She said stiffly, 'I don't think you understand, Kain. I organised this evening—I don't intend to leave until it's over.'

The two men with her exchanged looks. Without missing a beat, Mark said, 'And you've done it brilliantly, but everyone's going now, and if anything comes up I'll deal with it. Kain, have you met Tonia Guthrie?'

The artist, a thin, middle-aged woman with a narrow face and a furrowed forehead, looked irritated, but within a few seconds Kain's unforced magnetism had won her over so completely that she blurted, 'You know, I'm wishing I still did figure work! Have you ever posed? That superb bone structure would make for a magnificent portrait.'

He smiled. 'No, and I'm afraid I have no interest in having my portrait painted, but I think that's the nicest compliment I've ever had.'

The woman coloured, then laughed with him, clearly forgiving him for interrupting her talk with Mark.

Mark smiled benignly at them both. 'Great to see you here, Kain. Are we going to have your company at the auction?'

'I'm not sure, but there's always a chance.'

'I hope you can make it. Goodnight, Sable. And take tomorrow morning off—you've done a great job here, and you deserve it.'

'Thank you,' Sable said stiffly, furious with him for having his eyes fixed so firmly on the chance that Kain might buy one of the pictures that he'd sacrifice her.

Her thoughts were reinforced as they walked out to the door.

Kain said, 'Stop steaming, Sable. Your boss sees a mark and naturally he wants to cement some sort of interest. He might run a charitable foundation, but it's business and he needs the money to spend on the poor and voiceless.'

Instantly she flared into defence of her boss. 'It's very worthwhile—'

'Of course it is.' He looked down at her. 'And he's a damned good hustler.'

Outside in the sultry heat of an Auckland summer night, Sable ignored his words to say crisply, 'Tell me what this is all about, please. Is Brent all right?'

'Relax. Knowing Brent, he'll be enjoying himself very much. I don't know about you, but I haven't eaten for about nine hours. Come and have dinner with me.'

As though in answer her stomach chose just that moment to remind her uncomfortably that she'd only managed to snatch a handful of blueberries for her lunch.

His lips twitched. 'I suspected as much. There was something in the way you recommended those mushrooms that indicated a hollow inside you. I live by the Viaduct in a block with an excellent restaurant. Afterwards I'll take you home—or if it suits you better I'll order a taxi for you.'

Several more guests walked past them, their nods and smiles failing entirely to hide keen interest.

Sable hesitated, then mentally shrugged and gave in to curiosity. In spite of that urgent warning whisper from some primal instinct, eating dinner with him in a restaurant wouldn't put her in any sort of danger. 'Thank you—I am hungry.'

His apartment was in an art deco building that had once been a department store. Overlooking the harbour bridge and the Viaduct basin area with its waterfront restaurants and vibrant nightlife, the store had been rejuvenated with taste and flair—and a lot of money.

Kain indicated a bank of lifts, so the restaurant was upstairs, presumably to take advantage of the view. Sable noted the clever homage to the building's age, and more period details graced the foyer once they reached their destination. Eyeing a splendid bronze nymph carrying a torch, she repressed a grin. Tonight's featured artists would undoubtedly despise it, she thought cheerfully.

A niggle of apprehension made her tense when Kain took her arm and led her into a room—a large, superbly decorated living room.

After a swift, incredulous glance around she swung away from him, her face cold and still. 'This is your apartment,' she said icily, heading for the door.

He caught her arm, his fingers gripping just enough to stop her without bruising. 'Don't be so skittish. We need privacy.'

'You might—I don't,' she shot back, anger sharpening her voice. 'Let me go right now.'

'Not until you've heard what I have to say.'

CHAPTER THREE

KAIN caught Sable's free hand in a steely vice, almost paralysing the fingers that were folding into a serviceable fist. Grimly he said, 'Stop that right now. I'm not going to leap on you.'

His grip tightened a fraction, warning her not to pull away. Like enemies they stared at each other, dark eyes clashing with arctic grey, neither giving an inch.

Sable tried to concentrate on leaving. Right now. But all she could think of was Kain's nearness, the way he'd pulled her closer—so close her nostrils quivered at the faint, sexy smell that was his alone.

Although his gaze was flinty, she saw heat kindle in its depths, and shivered at the basic feminine knowledge that told her he wanted her.

She should be terrified.

Instead she felt a flare of wild exultation and had to fight a crazy impulse to take a step towards him— near enough to rest her head on his shoulder and feel the strength of his chest against her sensitised breasts.

Her body ached with keen, tantalising frustration and her lips felt hot and tender. She caught her breath and forced herself to say bleakly, 'Let me go.'

Kain released her. 'I'm sorry,' he said with curt brusqueness. 'That was unforgivable. I don't usually man-handle women.'

Her glare tried for contempt, but didn't quite make it beyond resentment. 'I'd hardly call it manhandling,' she said reluctantly.

Kain noticed less of her normal crispness in her tone, and he knew that the flash of hunger he'd seen in those mysterious eyes had been authentic.

And she, in her turn, had discerned his fierce response to her.

Sable's satiny skin invited a man's touch, and the red lips hinted at a recklessness that made him think of tangled sheets and long, long nights…

But what the *hell* was going on behind those steady, un-readable eyes? She was a very cool customer indeed, sexily chic in the sleek outfit of black and red that matched her hair and lips.

A stray, unwanted thought increased his annoyance at his unusual susceptibility.

What colour was the soft mouth beneath the gloss of lipstick? And when she creamed away the colour each night did all that controlled passion go with it?

Ignoring the unsubtle clamour in his body, he told her bluntly, 'If you really want to leave I'll organise a taxi for you.'

Somehow reassured by that—and thrilled in some primitively unregenerate part of her because for a moment she'd glimpsed the man behind the intimidating au-thority—Sable said, 'Oh, for heaven's sake, tell me what this is all about.'

One black brow rose. 'I will, but I'd like you to stay; I did promise to feed you, after all.' And he smiled.

Walk into my parlour, said the spider...

Sable blinked to keep her head from spinning. That wicked smile was wielded like a sword; he knew exactly how to disarm a woman.

If she had any sense at all she'd go.

An unusual recklessness persuaded her to say, 'First *I'd* like to know why you brought me here.'

And held her breath for his answer.

'Are you always this suspicious about being asked out to dinner?' Kain asked, his voice amused. Then his tone altered, and his broad shoulders lifted in a slight shrug. 'You looked pale and a little tired; I thought food was in order.'

Sable ignored the first question. 'I'm always pale—it's my natural colouring.'

'How are your iron levels?'

Her head came up with a jerk. Was he teasing? Yes, he was smiling. Coolly she said, 'They're fine, thank you.'

'Good.' He turned. 'I'll get a menu for you to look at.'

Sable glowered at his retreating back; effortlessly, with an authority that came from inner strength, Kain Gerard dominated every space he was in. He had that magical thing called charisma, the star quality that made everyone notice him.

OK, so his stunning good looks would automatically attract attention from women, but that compelling magnetism was based on his personality, not on his looks. He looked competent to the nth degree, as though he could deal with anything.

She envied him that inbuilt confidence; her own had been hard-won and was still precarious.

Did he take that constant attention and respect—the inviting, fascinated glances from women—for granted?

He'd be hell to love. There'd always be other women...

Embarrassed by the trend of her thoughts, she got to her feet and was turning towards the door when that tell-tale prickle at the back of her neck warned her he'd returned.

'Retreat, Sable?' His smile was idly mocking.

Feeling foolish, she said, 'No.'

After all, instinct told her that she didn't have to worry about her physical safety. Her emotional safety might be something else, but one meal wasn't going to overturn her life.

He held out a menu. 'Choose what you want for dinner, and when you've done that there's something you might like to see.'

'What?' Although she accepted the menu, she stayed stubbornly in place.

He touched a switch and the curtains glided back to reveal a terrace; she noted the satin gleam of a lap pool and the shimmering ebony curtain of water that fell into it.

'Look,' he said, indicating.

Sable gasped and walked across to stand beside him.

'It's one of the big cruise liners going out,' he told her. 'She's on her last voyage and this is her tribute to Auckland.'

'It could be a picture out of a fairytale.' Her voice was soft and wondering. Startled by her delight at the sight of the huge thing slipping silently down the harbour, decked with lights like a huge Christmas tree, she firmed her tone. 'A sight like that brings out the child in me.'

'How old are you?'

After a moment's hesitation she admitted, 'Twenty-six.'

'Six years younger than I am.' Together they watched the graceful relic of a more leisured age slide across the inky waters. 'Five thousand years of so-called civilisation haven't changed our basic natures. At heart we're the same as those ancestors who huddled around a fire for protection, and in all societies light means safety and security. Now, check that menu while I pour you a drink. Non-alcoholic, if you'd prefer it,' he added deadpan when she turned to refuse it.

Something equivocal in his tone alerted her, summoning instincts she'd long forgotten. Had he heard something about her father's addiction? Lightly she said, 'Actually, if you have it, a glass of lime and soda water would be wonderful.'

He produced that and handed it to her, waiting while she rapidly chose a dish. Then he left her again to deliver the order; she could hear his voice in the distance on the telephone. After a tiny sip of the refreshing drink she set the glass down on a table and looked around the room.

The penthouse wasn't anything like Brent's minimalist, decorator-driven apartment. Kain had clearly had input into the furnishings; its restrained luxury and strong lines fitted him.

He was frowning when he came back, a frown that deepened when she picked up her glass and held it in front of her like a pathetic shield. 'Come out onto the terrace,' he said.

How had he known that outside she could breathe more easily? She hadn't even realised it herself. Surrounded by the sounds and sights of a busy city she felt less restricted, more able to concentrate on the lush planting and the huge starry sky overhead than focus so completely on him.

They ate there as well. And, for all his forceful personality, Kain was surprisingly easy to talk to. Surprised, and a little alarmed, Sable realised she was speaking without thinking, and several times she suspected she might have given too much away.

So it was with an odd feeling of betrayal that she heard

him ask over coffee, 'Just what is your relationship with Brent?'

Loyalty to Brent drove her reply. 'I have no intention of discussing him behind his back.'

'I'm afraid you're going to have to.' Kain's tone—autocratic, completely uncompromising—chilled her.

Chin jutting, she demanded, 'Why?' *And how are you going to make me?*

He replied with formidable composure, 'Because if you and he are in love, I'll back off.'

Stunned, she stared at him. His smile stirred an unknown sensation deep inside her, a heat that beckoned, melting all her inhibitions in a fiery temptation.

Surely he couldn't mean…

'I'm not sure I understand.' Infuriatingly, her voice wobbled uncertainly, and the moment the words had emerged she wished she could call them back.

'It's quite simple,' he said, leaning back in his chair and surveying her with heavy-lidded eyes. 'I find you very attractive.'

His bluntness shocked and stirred her in equal measure. She could read nothing in his handsome face apart from enigmatic amusement, yet his eyes gave him away; beneath the lowered lids she discerned a glitter of desire.

An involuntary shiver—part fear, part keen anticipation that temporarily paralysed her thoughts—tightened her skin. For several increasingly taut seconds she dithered, finally saying with a hint of defiance, 'I'm not in love with Brent.'

Kain's expression didn't change except for a hardening of his gaze. 'So why is Brent convinced that he's in love with you?'

Sable really liked Brent, who seemed younger than his

years and oddly naïve; it was distasteful to be discussing him with his big, arrogant cousin. 'He knows how I feel,' she said steadily.

'I suspect he hopes he can change your mind.'

'He already knows it's not going to happen.' She hesitated, then said abruptly, 'I haven't ever given him any reason to feel that I'm interested in him other than as a friend.' It was as far as she was prepared to go.

'So moving into his apartment wasn't an indication that you were prepared to allow him certain privileges?'

His disbelieving tone made her lips tighten, and she said stiffly, 'No, he was being chivalrous. I had to leave my previous flat unexpectedly. I'm planning to be gone by the time he gets home, and he knows that.'

Kain examined her face, his cold eyes piercing and far too astute. Although she met that steady gaze without flinching, Sable was feeling very uncomfortable by the time he said, 'You're sure?'

'Absolutely sure.'

After another penetrating look he nodded as though making up his mind about something. 'I think the best way to deal with the situation is for you and me to become lovers.'

'What?' The word came out in a strangled squeak. The sounds of the city faded until all she could hear was the uneven, leaping thud of her heartbeats in her ears.

'Relax,' he advised, an ironic smile curving that beautiful, stern mouth. 'Just how far the supposed affair goes would be entirely up to you. I'm not suggesting we jump into bed in ten minutes' time.'

He watched swift heat scorch her delicate skin. So she could blush, could she? Strange that he should find it so intriguing.

Would she take the bait—*go for the billionaire in the bush rather than the millionaire in the hand*?

With a quick shake of her head, she said, 'That's an overreaction if ever I heard one. When he comes back he'll probably have met someone else to fancy himself in love with—'

'And if he hasn't?'

That made her pause, but she quickly recovered. 'He might be determined, but he's not going to *harass* me.' She gave him a direct look. 'Is he?'

'No.' Although Brent was good friends with his cousin, he refused to compete with him; finding Sable ensconced as Kain's mistress would put an automatic stop to any hopes he might have.

She said triumphantly, 'So there's no need for a fake love affair to persuade him that I'm not in love with him.'

His eyes gleamed, and he reached out a hand and snagged hers, drawing her to her feet. 'It doesn't need to be fake,' he said and bent his head and kissed her startled mouth.

It was a claim, open and demanding, and it smashed through her barriers with shaming ease. Later, thinking it over, Sable would blame her response on a wild rush of hormones to the brain, but right then she had no chance to think, no time to do anything but surrender to a compelling hunger that battered down her instinctive resistance.

Eventually he released her, his hands sliding down her arms and supporting her until her knees stiffened enough for her to be able to step away.

'That's not fake,' he said, his voice rough. 'Admit it, Sable—you want me every bit as much as I want you.'

Sable turned away from him, her thoughts tumbling disconnectedly around her brain, shattered to realise that her predominant emotion was humiliating frustration.

Never—*never*—had she felt like this before. She'd been content to keep her distance from men, walk alone through life, sure that somehow she'd missed out on the necessary hormones to summon passion.

How wrong she'd been!

Thinly, fighting to articulate clearly and without emotion, she managed to say, 'You might feel entitled to interfere in your cousin's life, but you have absolutely no right to meddle in mine.'

'Agreed,' he said calmly. 'But in this case your life and Brent's are entwined. And as your response told me you're telling the truth when you say you're not in love with him, why did you move in with him?'

Furious, she jerked around. Which was a mistake. The relentless judgement of his gaze hollowed out her stomach in something too close to panic for her to be able to sort out her thoughts.

With a desperate attempt at control, she said, 'I've already told you. When I had to leave my previous flat Brent offered me the use of his while he was away.'

Kain didn't say anything.

She glanced up, a faint hope freezing when her eyes met his unreadable ones. With an abrupt gesture she said, 'I'm still looking.'

'I can probably help you find—'

'No, thank you,' she jerked out, grabbing at the remnants of her pride.

In a tone close to insolence, he said, 'Cutting off your nose to spite your face is foolish. I'd thought better of you.'

A fresh spurt of humiliation drove her to blurt out, 'Are you trying to buy me off?'

His mouth curved in a humourless smile. 'No. If I were I'd be asking you to name your price.'

'Really? Surely such crude arrogance wouldn't fit in with your self image?' she suggested cuttingly.

Apparently genuinely amused, he laughed. 'Actually, there are times when only crude arrogance will do the trick. So you don't want to marry Brent?'

She said unevenly, 'It hasn't been discussed and I'd be very surprised to hear that Brent has any such plans.'

An evasive answer, Kain thought. She wasn't yet sure enough of him to give up on Brent.

Perhaps he should just seduce her.

His body sprang into action, pumping more hot blood through his veins. He reined it in. That testing kiss had proved one thing; her unrestrained passion meant she certainly wasn't in love with Brent.

But of course that didn't mean she wasn't planning to marry him.

And if that was what she wanted, unless someone intervened, she'd pull it off. According to his worried mother, Brent was besotted enough to offer marriage. Thirty thousand dollars worth of diamonds—definitely more than a casual gift—backed up Amanda's fears.

Startled by the dark anger that thought summoned, he flicked another glance across at Sable. She had a rare gift for stillness, her pure, remote profile etched against the darkness. She looked, he thought with a cold, biting irony, poised for flight.

A pose? If so it was well-chosen; it showed off her high breasts and the slender line of her legs. She was stunning enough to turn any man's head, let alone Brent's. His aunt had been right to worry about her son's relationship with Sable Jane Martin. Nothing Kain had learned about her made her in any way suitable for his cousin.

Kain ignored the uncomfortable stab of desire. He'd had

other casual lusts and not consummated them; a transient hunger wasn't important.

She could well be weighing up the monetary value of becoming his mistress as against being Brent's wife. Neither promised security; both would lead to profit and, if she was planning to become an events organiser, to a lucrative list of possible clients.

Mind made up, he said casually, 'I think it would certainly be a good idea for you to move out as soon as you can.'

He was agreeing with a decision she'd made before she'd even seen him. So why were her thoughts charging around her head, so that she felt both confused and oddly deflated? She turned her head and met his eyes, satirically watchful.

Did he ever lose that self-control? When he was making love, perhaps?

The intrusive, jagged edge of unease was banished by a slow curl of heat as her wayward mind summoned an image of him, bronzed and lean and powerful, bending towards her with a smile curving that beautiful mouth and his amazing ice-coloured eyes narrowed and intent...

Hands clenched at her sides, she consigned the image to the darkest reaches of her mind. She never had erotic fantasies—couldn't even remember ever dreaming about a man.

She certainly wasn't going to let Kain Gerard into her life. Even though he kissed like some sex god.

Especially because he kissed like some sex god.

Remember, she warned herself, what had happened afterwards: casually, almost unaffected, he'd stepped back from the heat and the fire and the torrid passion.

A sensible woman would run like hell.

Sable tried to assemble her thoughts into some rational pattern. Crisply she said, 'And although Brent might be young and inexperienced, he doesn't need a big cousin riding shotgun for him; he'll fall in love plenty of times before he finds someone he wants to spend the rest of his life with.'

'I couldn't agree more,' Kain said evenly, his lashes falling to hide his thoughts. He gave her a half-mocking smile. 'And as Brent doesn't mean anything more to you than a friend, we can move on from there.'

And just what did he mean by that? 'Move on?' She tired hard not to sound suspicious, but sensed she hadn't succeeded.

'Actually, we have moved on,' he said thoughtfully. 'I think that kiss was a definite advance, don't you?'

Furious, she realised her cheeks were hot again, but she stiffened her spine. If she didn't fight the reckless temptation to agree, this fierce attraction would lead to heartbreak.

Because Kain Gerard wasn't offering her anything beyond the satisfaction of lust.

She didn't need—or want—that.

Deliberately she said, 'I have a couple of likely prospects, so it won't be long before I leave the apartment.'

'Good.'

Something more had to be said. With every ounce of resolution she could muster, she added, 'But I'm not interested in an affair with you.' She paused, then added with too much emphasis, 'Not now, not ever.'

CHAPTER FOUR

KAIN looked speculatively at her for several seconds, then nodded, his expression giving nothing away. 'If that's what you really want.'

'What I really want is to go ho—*back*,' Sable corrected, because Brent's apartment had never been home.

He must have realised she was at the end of her tether. 'I'll take you.'

'No.'

But he did, even seeing her to the door. 'Goodnight,' he said with an ironic smile she resented, and watched her unlock the door with the personalised key Brent had given her.

He didn't come in, for which she was profusely grateful. But once inside she noticed the pile of newspapers she'd left unread while she'd scanned the ads for flatmates.

Reluctantly she sorted through them, hesitating when she came to the one announcing pictures from the racing carnival. 'Oh, stop being such a wuss,' she said aloud, and spread it out on the table, giving a soft dismayed hiss as she saw the photograph of her and Kain.

It couldn't have been more damning; the photographer had caught the moment of challenge between them, when they'd been staring at each other like two people in the first stages of blatant sexual infatuation.

No wonder Poppy had been giving her speculative looks all week! Kain photographed superbly, those slashing cheekbones and lethal mouth, the narrowed eyes... Shivering, she remembered his kiss, and the slow, silky desire that had streamed through her at the touch of his tongue.

'Just remember,' she warned that sneaky inner wanton soberly, 'he might look like a god, but he has all the instincts of a shark.'

Driven by anger and a humiliating sense of betrayal, she folded the newspapers and dumped them in the recycling bin. At least it was the weekend; she gave a wry smile. She had two whole days to hide out before she had to face more of Poppy's unspoken curiosity!

Next morning she ate fruit and toast and drank one more than her usual cup of coffee before getting up and starting on the small amount of housework. The apartment was serviced, but she had clothes to wash. And once they were done she'd have to resume her search for another apartment to share.

Half an hour later she opened the Saturday paper and started the dreary process, only to be interrupted by the warble of her cell phone. Frowning, she answered it.

'I've just had a call from the Browns,' her boss, Mark Russell, said without preliminaries, his tone warning her she wasn't going to like what he had to say.

Sable frowned, her stomach hollowing. The Browns were the couple who'd lent their showpiece mansion for the auction and showings. 'And?'

'They've had bad news and can't let us have the auction at their place.'

Horrified, she took in a deep breath. Don't show terror,

she reminded herself. In her calmest voice she said, 'I'm so sorry about that. What—'

'But they've suggested another venue—even better!'

Hugely relieved in spite of the massive amount of work this would entail—and only a week to do it in!—Sable let out a silent huff of breath. 'Whose? And where is it?'

'Kain Gerard has offered us his place at Mahurangi.' Her boss's voice oozed satisfaction. 'It couldn't be more perfect.'

She froze, wondering wildly how this had happened. 'Mahurangi is an hour's drive north of here,' she objected without thinking. 'Will people want to go that far?'

'Oh, yes, especially as it means seeing one of the finest Gothic Revival houses still standing in New Zealand—if not *the* finest. Totara Bay homestead is magnificent. And then there's the cachet of the Gerard name. Very exclusive.' He rolled the last two words around his mouth like the first sip of a fine wine.

Controlling her dismay, Sable set her mind to work. Delivering the goods was the benchmark of success in the events business. Mark's comment had sounded snobbish, but she knew what he meant. The success of the auction relied on pulling in as many of the country's rich as they could—both *nouveau* and Old Money.

Kain Gerard moved in very grand circles on the world stage, and for one night competitive, status-seeking people could feel they belonged in them. They already had almost a hundred and fifty people registered for the auction—once this news got out there would be more.

Infusing her voice with enthusiasm, she said, 'Yes, of course. Because it's an invited audience, we can use buses to pick people up from their homes and deliver them back.' She grabbed a pen and started to scribble notes. 'The Fleet line

huve about half a dozen luxury coaches—I'll get them if I
have to beg on my knees for them. All right, leave it to me.'

'Kain has given me a contact number.' He read it out carefully. 'I realise this is going to take a lot of time to organise,
so take as much time off as you need to get it done. And I'll
contact the insurance agents and the security firm for you.'

Five minutes later she put the cell phone down and sat
staring into space. It took the summons of the apartment
telephone to get her moving again. 'Hello,' she said
without identifying herself.

Kain Gerard said on an amused note, 'I hope I didn't
wake you.'

'No.' She'd known it would be him.

'I assume you've heard from Russell.'

'Yes.'

'I thought we could drive up to the house so you could
inspect it.'

Sable most emphatically did not want to go there with
him, but she had no choice. She said politely, 'Thank you,
that would be great if you can spare the time.'

'When?'

'This morning?'

'Of course. I'll pick you up in half an hour.'

'Just one thing—is the lawn at Totara Bay big enough to
hold a marquee that will take a couple of hundred people?'

'Yes,' he said, his laconic tone stopping a note away
from another *of course*.

'Right, I'll be ready.'

She cast a harried glance at the newspaper as she hung
up. So much for untangling herself from Brent; tomorrow
she'd ring around the rest of the suitable ads, she promised
herself, knowing that by the next morning the best places
would be gone.

In the meantime pride insisted she do something about the shadows beneath her eyes. It took a heavy application of concealing stick to hide the evidence of her restless night, but by the time Kain Gerard drove into the parking area she was ready for him, walking towards his car before he had a chance to get out.

Stomach knotting, she got into the front seat, gave him her coolest, personal-assistant smile, and said pleasantly, 'This is extremely kind of you.'

He set the car in motion again, lean hands confident on the wheel as he manoeuvred it out of the parking area. 'Anything for a good cause,' he said on a sardonic inflection.

She didn't speak while they drove through the busy morning city; although the tension inside her tightened her nerves unbearably, she much preferred that to conversation that seemed more like a fencing bout than an exchange of views.

But when they'd left the harbour bridge behind and were purring along the motorway he told her, 'I'll be overseas for a couple of days during the week, so you'll liaise with my housekeeper. Do you have a car?'

'No,' she admitted reluctantly.

He shrugged. 'I'd have thought one was necessary for this sort of thing.'

'It's only a sideline so far,' she explained without expression, 'and previously I've always worked in Auckland.' Where there were plenty of buses, and taxis for late at night.

'Mark Russell says you have a definite knack for it.' He sounded amused, as though events management was a nice little hobby.

She refused to bristle. 'I hope so. This will be a real test for me.'

'I'm sure you'll deal admirably with it,' he said suavely.

The kiss that had haunted her dreams was a weight on her mind—alluring, forbidden, summoning a fierce response that still simmered through her body. The memory lay like a challenge between them, so that she even wondered if Kain had somehow engineered this latest development.

And dismissed the idea. Mark had mentioned that the Browns, a nice couple, had had some bad news. Sometimes coincidences just seemed to set themselves up with deliberate malice.

She kept her gaze fixed ahead, watching the asphalt unravel in front of them as they passed from the city into the countryside, green and verdant, and then quickly came out onto the coast.

Silence stretched uncomfortably between them, a silence she refused to break. Kain would win any contest of wills because he held all the power, but she could at least give him a run for it.

A little later they turned off the highway and began a winding journey down a peninsula. Glimpses of the sea and a mangrove-fringed estuary began to appear between the hills, and finally, after five minutes' descent through a thick pall of native forest, they emerged into sunlight that made her blink.

The sign on the open gates said simply Totara Bay. The drive led through superb grounds, and as they came through the garden her question about the size of the lawn came back to haunt her. No wonder he'd sounded amused! Backed by trees, the lawns seemed to go on for infinity bathed in a shimmering brilliance of light. Close by— probably hidden by the thick screen of huge pohutukawa trees—was a beach.

Her breath caught in her throat as the house came into

view. Big, serenely gracious, it was a picture-book homestead painted white with a grey roof. To her horror and
alarm, Sable's eyes filled with strange, lost tears, so that
she had to blink furiously and furtively as they approached
the front door.

She felt a deep connection, as though she'd come home.
Emotions she'd thought long conquered stirred deep inside
her—the childish yearning for security, for beauty that
lasted, for stability and peace—everything she'd envied,
longed for, when she was growing up.

All here, in this house, owned by this man who threatened her hard-won composure, her very view of herself.

Terrified at the thought of revealing just how much it
affected her, Sable asked, 'How old is this beautiful
building?'

'About a hundred and twenty years. My great-great-
great-grandfather settled here almost a hundred and fifty
years ago.' He stopped the car on the gravel in front of the
big entrance. 'I grew up here.'

Old Money. No, make that Very Old Money. She knew
about Very Old Money; the memory still stung of the
woman who'd descended on the school when she'd been
about eight and demanded without lowering her voice that
her child be removed from sitting beside Sable.

She'd known why. The daughter of the town drunk had
no place beside a child with an Old Money background.
And this superbly maintained house emphasised as
nothing else could the distance between her and Kain,
even in egalitarian New Zealand.

She could feel Kain's glance on her averted face, sharp
and far too perceptive. Stonily she said, 'What a perfect
setting for the auction.' She dragged her eyes from the superb
façade. 'I assume there'll be plenty of parking for the buses.'

'Buses?'

She managed a rather patronising smile. 'Don't worry—we won't be bussing in thousands of people. As you know this is an invitation-only occasion, and at the most there will be half a dozen vehicles—no more.' For some reason she asked, 'Have you decided yet whether you're going to attend?'

He gave her a narrow glance. 'Of course. This is my home.'

His words neatly nailed the yawning gap between them. He got out, his long legs taking him swiftly around to open the door for her. Clutching her briefcase, Sable went with him around the side of the house to a wide gravel parking area.

She looked around and nodded. In a voice she hoped sounded brisk and businesslike, she said, 'Yes, perfect for buses.'

The interior was as beautiful as the exterior, but Sable concentrated on not staring too obviously. Although many old houses were gloomy, this one had been skilfully renovated at some stage to let in the light, and it was furnished with a magnificent mixture of old and new pieces.

The art was magnificent too. No postmodernism, she noted with an inward irony, just an eclectic collection of masterpieces, some by minor artists—and some, she thought as her gaze lingered on the proud, passionate face of a woman dressed in full Victorian regalia, by definitely major talents.

An ancestor, no doubt about it; that unknown woman and Kain shared the same arrogantly aristocratic bone structure.

Kain took her into a large room that opened out onto a wide veranda. 'I suggest you serve the cocktails and canapés here. People can come in through those French doors and then take their drinks out into the marquee for the actual auction. And serving food here in the salon will be easier for the caterers.'

He was taking over, she realised, and without even thinking about it. That authority was as essential a part of him as the arrogant jut of his jaw and the strong features that made him the most handsome man she'd ever met.

A quiver of heat in the pit of her stomach warned her not to go there. Speaking a little too quickly, she asked, 'What's your kitchen like? Sometimes it's simpler for the caterers to set up a mobile canteen.'

'You'd better inspect it.'

Again that amused note in his voice, a note she understood when saw the kitchen. No ordinary farm kitchen this, she realised. The homestead kitchen had been set up for cooking for crowds.

'There'll be no problem here,' she agreed, her gaze ranging past a vast and very modern range to an industrial-size dishwasher. 'It's perfect. I imagine you have plenty of water.'

'We do. Come and see where the marquee will go.'

Natural, inborn authority was all very well, she thought mutinously, but the marquee would go where *she* wanted it.

Nevertheless, she turned to follow him, only to find he hadn't moved. Although she tried to pull her step, nothing could stop her from cannoning into him. Stunned, she dropped her briefcase, groped for it wildly, and found herself lurching too close to a fall.

He hauled her upright. She thought she heard him say something above the thunder of her pulse. And then his arms tightened. She looked up.

And every instinct shrieked a warning—*run*!

Except for the more basic need that held her mesmerised, her eyes widening as they took in the smoky grey of his. He smiled and lowered his head. Unable to think, Sable let her lashes drift down.

She expected the same sort of kiss as that first one— devouring, challenging—but this one settled so lightly on her mouth she barely felt it beyond an extra warmth, a slow, sinfully decadent caress of lips against lips, so tantalising she had to fight the urge to let herself give free rein to the hunger building inside her.

In spite of the turmoil of fears and commands that tore her mind, her body knew very well where it wanted to be— locked in Kain's arms, his faint, intensely erotic scent homing straight to hidden receptors in her brain.

Breathlessly she waited for something—though she didn't know what.

'Sable.' Her name against her mouth caressed her ears, his deep voice roughened by an exciting hint of raw passion.

Her heart jumped at the subtly erotic way he spoke, and jumped again when he commanded, 'Say my name.'

It seemed far too intimate a gesture, a kind of surrender Sable wasn't ready to make.

If only she could think straight she'd know why. Alarmed, she opened her eyes and met his, their arctic frigidity banished by the intense flame of arousal.

A clamour of desire fountained up through her, ferociously sweeping away every commonsense thought in its heady passage. She should refuse, or taunt him by calling him Mr Gerard…

But need burned hard and hot and fierce in her, a powerful hunger more compelling than her cowardice. Yielding, she said huskily, 'Kain.'

However, because some weakly sane part of her didn't want him to realise how this teasing seduction stripped away her defences, she added, 'Gerard.'

Watching his name play on her lips, he laughed softly. 'My name has never looked so good.'

And then he kissed her again.

Every coherent thought disappeared in the raw response his kiss summoned, so removed from any previous experience that Sable capitulated without a pang of fear or concern. Lost in a turmoil of carnal craving, she dimly recognised she'd never felt safer—as though nothing in the world could touch her when she was in Kain's arms.

Until he stiffened and lifted his head, releasing her. Dazed by the sudden coldness of space between them, she stared mutely up at him, but he was looking over her head.

So quietly only she could have heard him, he said, 'Someone's coming.'

She stepped back, almost tripping over her briefcase, and hastily bent to pick it up, cravenly grateful for something to do that would get her even for a moment out of his scrutiny.

From behind, a pleasant middle-aged female voice said, 'Oh—sorry, Kain. I didn't realise you were in here.'

'Miss Martin is checking out the kitchen,' he said smoothly.

Sable straightened up, hoping to heaven that any extra colour in her face would be attributed to bending. She met a pair of blue eyes, direct and interested, and a warm smile.

'Sable, this is Helen Dawson,' Kain continued. 'Helen, this is Sable Martin, the events planner for the art auction. She thought the caterers might prefer to bring a mobile canteen here, so I brought her in to show her they don't need to.'

'We can deal with caterers,' his housekeeper said with conviction.

'I can see that.' Yes, her voice sounded quite normal— well, at least to someone who didn't know her very well.

She just hoped her mouth didn't reveal that it had been

soundly kissed—and kissing—a few seconds ago. Colouring slightly, she told her heart to slow down and added wryly, 'I've seen commercial kitchens that were less well-equipped than this one.'

'Homestead kitchens were built to be ready for anything,' the housekeeper said crisply. 'Although nowadays we no longer kill all our own meat, and we have to give away most of the fruit and vegetables because there isn't a family in the homestead to eat the produce.' She grinned at her employer. 'Kain's got a good appetite, but he's just not here enough.'

Teasingly Kain said, 'Helen is dying for the day she can cook for ten again as a regular thing.'

'Ten?' Sable laughed ruefully. 'The foster home I lived in for a year could have done with someone like you.'

The housekeeper looked startled, then thoughtful. 'I'm sure,' she said, 'but they probably couldn't afford me.'

She and Sable exchanged glances, and Sable felt that she'd found an ally.

With a quick nod the housekeeper said, 'Is there anything you'd like to know?'

Sable took out her notes. 'If we could go through these,' she suggested.

To her relief Kain left them to it. Half an hour later, convinced that the housekeeper was not only competent but actively helpful, Sable closed her notebook. 'Thanks a lot. I'm feeling much better about everything now.'

'I suppose a cancellation so close to the date is every event planner's nightmare,' the housekeeper observed.

'One of them.' She gave another smile. 'I'm actually moonlighting at this. I work for the Russell Foundation as a PA in my real life.'

'Which do you prefer?'

Sable said thoughtfully, 'I like working for the Foundation—it's satisfying in a moral way.' That sounded pretentious so she hurried on, 'But I must confess that in spite of the numerous hassles this is much more creative. I really enjoy it.'

'Like the difference between a good plain dinner for a family and a gourmet dinner of ten courses for foodies.' The housekeeper nodded. 'I wouldn't like to have to do either all the time, but I do like a challenge. So does Kain. Right from the time he was born.'

It sounded like a warning, one Sable instinctively understood. Hoping that the warmth over her cheekbones wasn't too obvious, she said cheerfully, 'At the moment the only challenge I'm interested in is providing such a great evening that the punters will spend all the money they can afford on the art.'

'I'm sure you'll do that.' The older woman looked past her. 'I think we've got everything organised here, Kain.'

'Good.' His voice was without inflection. 'Sable, you'd better come and check out the rest of the place.'

A cool undernote to his words sent a chill down her spine. The air seemed heavy with warnings right now, Sable thought, knowing she was overreacting. She knew why; when she was with Kain Gerard her every sense was honed and more acute as though he set off subliminal alarms in her.

He took her back to the salon and out through the wall of French doors onto the verandah, a long, wide, covered area that led down onto a lawn.

'The marquee will be set up here,' he said, indicating.

After a rapid inspection of the perfect sward of grass bordered by an exotic mix of subtropical and native plantings, Sable nodded. 'Yes, this is ideal. How do you want the guests corralled?'

'Do you think that's necessary?'

She shrugged. 'We don't want them wandering off and getting so interested in your fabulous gardens—or each other—that they forget they're here to spend money.'

'Of course not,' he said cynically. 'Are you always so single-minded?'

'I'm paid to be,' she told him, her voice cool and verging on the abrupt.

Let him think what he liked—sure, she'd never lived in the death-dealing poverty that the Foundation clients overseas suffered daily, but she knew what life was like for those on the bottom of the heap. It wouldn't hurt over-wealthy status-seekers to dig deeply into their pockets.

'And I'm sure you try to give good value.'

She met that assessing gaze with brittle composure. 'It doesn't pay to short-change the people I make a living from.'

He gave a short laugh. 'Honest too.'

Sable hoped he hadn't noticed her flinch. He'd never know just how much those casual words hurt! Burying ugly memories, she said, 'Naturally. Now, about marking off the grounds—a length of white-painted picket fencing would look appropriate here and could be fixed to the trellis of that archway, stopping access to the rest of the garden. There will be security, of course.'

'I'll use my own,' he said.

Startled, she said, 'But I've already organised the firm we always use—'

'Cancel them,' he said indifferently.

She said, 'We've signed a contract—'

Kain's eyes were as cold as the depths of space. 'Then pay them, but I'm using my own security men.' And when she started a further protest he said quietly, 'This is not negotiable, Sable.'

He had her in a cleft stick and he knew it. With the auction only a week away she hadn't a chance of finding another venue as suitable as this.

Although she was seething, she gave in with as much grace as she could muster. 'If it's so important to you, then all right.'

'I won't charge you, and I assume you've only paid a deposit to the firm you use. This way there'll be more money for the Foundation beneficiaries. And my men will take their orders from me,' he ended coolly.

Everything in Sable rebelled at his tone, but she nodded. 'Do you want me to organise the picket fence?'

'No, I'll do that.'

Directing a false, meaningless smile at his chin, she made a production of closing the notebook she'd been using. 'Right, I think I've got everything I need. Now, if you don't mind I'd like to go back to Auckland so I can start ringing people.'

'I suggest we have lunch first,' he said. 'Helen has prepared a meal for us in the gazebo.'

Something had changed. Kain had changed.

No, she was fantasising. She didn't know him well enough to be able to see behind the handsome mask of his features.

Yet her stomach performed an odd little lurch. Concentrate, she ordered her body. Try focusing on how downright arrogant he is. Did he get off on ordering people about? Probably.

But the memory of those kisses burned through her, daring her to enjoy this time with him, to take up the challenge he presented—to see what he'd be like as a lover.

Common sense warned Sable that though he'd be superb, in the end she'd get badly hurt. Tonelessly she said, 'How kind. Thank you.'

The gazebo was modern, and overlooked a crescent of beach as white as a quarter moon. It was utterly beautiful and empty of people—no public access here, Sable realised, letting her eyes skim an elegant yacht moored in the bay.

How the very, very, *very* rich lived, she thought snidely, and turned to inspect the gazebo, set up for relaxed entertaining with luxurious loungers and a long table that hinted at many guests. Someone—the housekeeper?—had collected flowers and arranged them in a huge white conch shell that set off burnished petals shimmering in the passionate colours of high summer.

Kain said, 'If you'd like to wash your hands there's a cloakroom here.'

And sure enough, to one side was a very luxurious changing shed and shower for swimmers, so they wouldn't track sand into that opulent house.

She glanced at herself in the mirror and almost gasped. Her mouth was red and soft, her skin glowing, and her eyes as dark and hot as coals—a dead giveaway. Heedless of her carefully applied cosmetics, she splashed her skin with cold water, closing her eyes as she blotted it dry and tried to summon the most calming thoughts she could.

It didn't work. She opened her eyes and stared defiantly at her reflection. OK, so she'd been completely and shamefully *stupid*. Instinct told her that in spite of Kain's arrogance, if she'd demanded he stop kissing her, he would have.

But for the first time in her life she'd actually experienced desire, so she'd let him. Not only *allowed* it to happen, she thought, more colour heating her skin, she'd co-operated with humiliating enthusiasm.

And now he knew for certain that she wanted him.

She set her jaw and looked her reflection straight in the eye.

It wasn't ever going to happen again. She'd make sure he understood that from now on any relationship between them would be purely professional. And if he didn't get the unspoken message she'd tell him with as much starchy assurance as she could summon.

But first she had to get through this lunch. The thought of eating with him closed her throat.

So where's that *professional* attitude? she taunted her reflection, and held her head high, stiffening her shoulders as she turned to walk back to Kain.

She would *not* be intimidated by him or his wealth or his social position. Or by the fact that when he looked at her, touched her, she went up in flames of lust.

CHAPTER FIVE

AFIRE with determination, Sable strode out of the changing room. In that exquisite folly of a gazebo a meal had appeared on the table—a superb summer lunch of courgette flowers puffed out by a stuffing, and mussels, served with fresh home-baked rolls still warm from the oven, plus a salad.

'Wine?' Kain asked.

'No, thank you.' But she was surprised when he didn't pour himself a glass. Brightly she said, 'This looks delicious.'

'Helen was a bit worried in case you didn't eat seafood, but I remembered that last night you chose scallops for dinner.'

The fact that he'd remembered made her oddly uneasy. 'I like all seafood,' she said neutrally, and steered the conversation towards the auction.

Through lunch—which tasted as good as it looked—her unease increased. She was sure there'd been a subtle but discernible shift in his attitude towards her. His reservation, tinged with an all-too-human male awareness, had morphed into something more intimidating.

And telling herself that she was imagining things didn't help.

Not that she cared what he thought of her, she decided stoutly, accepting a slice of succulent peach pie. Just for the hell of it she topped it with some of the whipped cream Kain passed to her. She needed all the support she could get.

But when they'd finished eating and she was enjoying the tea she'd asked for instead of the coffee he was drinking, he said without preamble, 'Now, tell me why you left your first job.'

At first Sable didn't—*couldn't*—believe she'd heard what he'd said. 'What?' she asked blankly, fighting for control.

He was watching her with relentless eyes behind those astonishing lashes. 'After you left school, you were given an office job by an elderly solicitor. However, you left in a hurry and under a cloud.'

'I didn't,' she said tonelessly, clasping her hands in her lap as sick horror washed over her.

One black brow revealed his disbelief. 'So what happened?'

Humiliated, she held her head high and met cold grey eyes with a direct challenge. 'The job was purely temporary—Mr Frensham knew I planned to go on to study for a business degree. Which I did.'

'After you'd seduced his grandson. As insurance, I suppose, in case Frensham found out what you'd done.' A sardonic smile hardened his face even further. 'The grandson must have felt a total idiot when you dumped him. Apparently he was a broken man.'

Sable fought back the debilitating feeling of being tainted, the shattering knowledge that he'd sent someone to check up on her, someone who'd snooped around, stirring up gossip again.

That had to explain the subtle change in him; while she'd

been conferring with Helen Dawson, he must have—what? Taken a telephone call from a firm of private detectives?

Her skin crawled. At least he'd never find out what had really happened. Everyone involved in that sordid business was, as far as she knew, dead, except for Derek—and she hadn't seen Derek since she'd realised how he'd used and betrayed her.

She remained stubbornly silent, eyes black in her white face, her cheekbones suddenly prominent above a mouth held under tight control.

Kain tamped down a sudden, wild urge to shake the truth from her. He goaded, 'You were lucky to get away with a spot of forgery—if that's all it was—but I'm afraid I'll feel obliged to tell Brent about your somewhat chequered past. Of course I can't guarantee that he won't tell others.'

'Or that *you* won't,' she flashed, eyes glittering. 'I don't give a damn who you tell. You can't prove anything.'

'Mud sticks.' He'd deliberately used the word forgery to see if she reacted. He'd seen her lashes flicker, but she hadn't corrected him.

Why would she? Forgery was almost honourable compared to blackmail—and the subsequent suicide of one of her victims.

Coldly, ruthlessly, he went on, 'If this becomes common knowledge it would make the Russell Foundation rethink your position with them. After all, they deal with huge amounts of money and in the charity business image is everything. To protect themselves I imagine you could be asked to resign.'

That got to her. Her mouth trembled until she firmed it, only her eyes proclaiming her defiance. 'I did not commit forgery.'

'Then what did you do?'

Great dark eyes glared at him. 'Nothing but be in the wrong place at the wrong time,' she said harshly.

She almost convinced him. Get a grip, Kain told himself with harsh determination. She'd only been seventeen then, but she was older and tougher now and she had Brent and his millions in her sights. Accepting that diamond ring meant she was serious about taking him for what she could.

Yet in spite of everything, dammit, he wanted her!

His broad shoulders lifted. 'Of course, if they've got any sense they'll point out that part of their brief is to help those who are in strife. They could hold you up as an example of someone they've helped to turn her life around.'

The last vestiges of colour drained from her face. 'I loathe you,' she said, every word sharp and clear and fierce.

'Yes, I thought you'd hate that,' he returned coolly. 'In spite of everything, you've got pride.'

'*Because* of everything I've got pride,' she returned.

It had taken her a lot of work to achieve it; she'd started out with none. Humiliation corroded her, but she had to convince him that she was innocent. Desperate, she hurried on, 'I took nothing, forged nothing. Trust me, if I'd done anything illegal I'd have been prosecuted. I wasn't. Doesn't that tell you something?'

Eyes coldly dispassionate, he examined her as though she was something slimy and despicable, and when he spoke it was with ruthless precision. 'Only that it would hurt too many people to have to give evidence in open court.' She stared mutely at him as he pressed his advantage. 'If I'm forced—by your intransigence—to reveal your dirty little secret, I don't need to tell you how difficult it will be for you to get any decent job in New Zealand.'

He had the power to make good on his threat. New Zealand was small, its business communities closely linked, and it would take a unique HR department to overlook his accusation.

All her hard-won savings had gone; she literally had no money to go anywhere else, not even to Australia. Without a job she'd have no way of saving more.

Ruthlessly he went on, 'And of course it will mean the end of your sideline as an events planner.'

'No! There's no reason—' Her shocked voice dwindled into silence as she gazed at his impervious face. Of course it would be the end—an end to *all* her hopes and plans.

'Surely you don't expect anyone to trust a woman with a past like yours?' he enquired silkily.

Sable fought back a corrosive, futile sense of betrayal. It hurt in a previously invulnerable part of her that it should be Kain who was doing this to her. Somehow in the short time since they'd met he'd penetrated her defences and reached her on another, deeper level than the purely physical.

She said stonily, 'What do you want?'

'I think you know.'

Sable met his implacable gaze—steady, merciless— and realised sickly that she had no option. Her head came up. Flatly, tasting the bitterness of defeat, she said, 'So what are your terms?'

His lashes drooped, hiding any emotion. 'You move in with me. You pretend to be in love with me.'

The pretty little gazebo suddenly seemed like a prison, narrowing around Sable.

'That's impossible,' she said thinly.

'Nothing is impossible.' His voice was deliberate and relentless. 'If you're honest about not wanting Brent, this will be the simplest and least painful way for him to give up on you.'

Emotions rioting through her, Sable realised she was wringing her hands, their movements revealing her tumultuous, panicky thoughts. Stilling them she said urgently, 'You run the risk of having him hate you. Family feuds lasting for generations have been founded on incidents less painful than that.'

'He doesn't hold grudges.' He watched her with a clinical lack of compromise as he finished cynically, 'And who can fight true love?'

'No.' Frantically Sable tried to control her rioting thoughts. She needed to get away somewhere—anywhere she could think without his presence scrambling her brain. 'It's a crazy idea, absolutely crazy. And even if it works, it can only make things harder for Brent.'

'In the short term, possibly,' Kain conceded, but then with a calm authority she found infuriating he went on, 'I always consider the long-term situation.'

She fought the unnerving feeling of being mercilessly backed into a corner, herded into a situation she could never control. 'I can't believe you've even considered it.'

'It won't be so bad.' He spoke without emphasis, eyes never leaving her face. 'It will involve some play-acting—but I'm sure you'll cope. And as my lover you'll be living in luxury. You'll need clothes, of course, and money—'

'I don't want anything from you,' she said between her teeth.

'The labourer is worthy of her hire,' he returned sardonically. 'Think of it as an all-expenses paid holiday.'

How could he be so cruel when he was toying with her life, her future? Sable got to her feet. In a thick, angry tone, she said, 'No. No, I won't do it.'

He leaned back in his chair and examined her with narrowed eyes. 'Sit down.' When she stayed stubbornly upright he repeated in a steely voice, 'Sit down.'

'I feel better standing,' she said brusquely, forcing her chin upwards, and then fell silent, unable to find words to express her outrage.

Nevertheless, she was glad of the emotion because it banished—temporarily—the darkness of betrayal.

And that was stupid, because she'd known right from the start that his kisses meant nothing...

'Forget the past.' His cool insolence grated unbearably on her overstretched nerves. 'It's the future I'm concerned with.'

But when she took an involuntary step backwards he said in the same level voice, 'Think carefully before you make your final decision.'

Fighting a debilitating indecision, she scanned the hard, handsome face while her mind hesitated over equally painful choices. She could see no way out. In a low, fierce voice, she stated, 'I won't sleep with you.' It was surrender, but at least she could salvage some pride.

'Your decision,' he returned with an indifferent shrug. 'Of course, in return for your co-operation I'll keep silent about your past.'

'So you're offering me a few weeks of luxury—just until your cousin comes back and gives up on any chance of marrying me—for my future?' She didn't even try to hide her scorn and frustration.

'That seems an overdramatic way of looking at it,' he drawled. 'People like you always fall on their feet.' He stood up, towering over her, his gaze as arrogant as the formidable contours of his face. 'So what's your decision?'

Sable sent him a bitter look, wishing she had the

courage to throw his obscene deal in his face and walk out
of there with some shred of honour left. 'I don't have any
option, do I?'

'There are always options,' he said ironically. 'Do I
take that as an agreement?'

He was going to force her to say it.

Bleakly, angrily, she muttered, 'Yes.'

Again she was subjected to a dispassionate, calculating
survey. 'Be aware I don't take kindly to broken agree-
ments,' he told her. 'Now sit down and finish your tea.'

After a few seconds of staring mutely at his implacable
face she sat down, but of course she couldn't manage to
drink anything. Her throat had closed, and she sat without
speaking as she stared out across the estuary, clinging to
her composure by a grim effort of will.

She had no way of proving her innocence. Even when
he'd apologised for misjudging her, old Mr Frensham had
never revealed how he'd discovered that it had been his
grandson who'd tried to blackmail some of his clients.
Only her knowledge of her own innocence, and Derek's
abrupt departure from the village had convinced her of the
identity of the perpetrator.

Where Derek was now she had no idea; the thought of
seeing him again filled her with disgust. No doubt Kain
could find him, she thought with a touch of hysteria that
frightened her. But no doubt he'd looked no further than
the daughter of the town drunk.

Mr Frensham had known her all her life, but he hadn't
believed her when she'd denied using his files to blackmail
his clients.

Kain's kisses still burnt through her body, yet they'd
been nothing more than a cynical exercise in power and
control on his part.

Breaking the silence, he said calmly, 'I'll take you back to Brent's apartment to pack.'

She got to her feet, refusing to ask whether he planned to imprison her here or in his penthouse.

The trip back to Auckland was without conversation; she wished he'd turn the radio on so that she wouldn't feel quite so threatened by the silence.

He didn't leave her in the apartment. Once inside he said, 'I have a call to make.'

At least he wasn't planning to monitor her while she packed, she thought bitterly, heading for the room she'd been using.

But once there she stood indecisively, her mind racing without result.

Kain thought she was a fraudster and a cheat...

He knew she went weak at the knees when he touched her, and he'd had no hesitation using that weakness against her. Her stomach hollowed. She faced a future that seemed unimaginably bleak, held to a decision she had been black-mailed into, because of something she'd never done.

The door opened and he came into the room.

Sable's gaze flicked across his unreadable face. After taking a deep breath she asked unemotionally, 'Why?'

When he lifted one black brow she expanded, 'Why is it necessary that I move in with you? We've only just met—are you such a fast mover in all your relationships?'

'No, but this one is different.' His smile was mocking. 'This is true love, remember.'

A sinuous little chill scudded the length of her spine. 'And what's going to happen when it all falls through? All the lies will be obvious.'

'It won't matter much once Brent is well and truly over you, because he won't care then. Until that happens you'll be my recognised live-in lover.' He looked around, frowning, then fixed her with a diamond-sharp gaze. 'I don't share, and neither does Brent. Although we're good mates he's always been slightly envious of me. He's not going to like the fact that you've moved in with me, but he'll probably blame you for that, not me.'

'Thanks a lot,' she said unevenly.

He said, 'I could just tell him about your larcenous habits. He happens to be honest.'

She turned away, her hands clenched at her side.

Kain's voice hardened even further. 'Get moving. I'll help you pack.'

'You will not!'

But when she still didn't stir he strode towards the wardrobe and opened it.

'Hey,' she began, racing after him. When he ignored her she said between her teeth, 'Touch anything and I'll—I'll—'

His smile was pure male challenge, tight and cold and fierce. 'You'll what? Hit me? Try it, Sable.'

Backed into a corner, she forced herself to surrender to a will even stronger than hers. 'All right, I'll pack. Just get out!'

'I'll wait in the hall,' he said laconically and walked out.

While she stuffed clothes into her old backpack and grabbed her sponge bag and cosmetics, Sable thought vengefully how she'd so enjoy shattering that domineering, arrogant male stance he used to impose his will on someone else!

Her hands faltered while she zipped up the bag.

Except that he was in the position of power so she'd never have the chance. Setting her jaw, she picked up her pack and marched out into the hall.

Kain swung around the moment she came through the

door. Without saying anything he held out his hand, and Sable gave him the backpack. Clearly carrying something for a woman was an automatic reaction.

She said curtly, 'I'm not giving up my job.'

'I don't believe I've suggested you do so,' he returned. 'Is this all?'

'Yes.' Not a lot for five years of earning, but she'd shopped carefully and saved every cent she could. Just as well…

'You travel light,' he observed.

She stopped. 'I need to clean out the fridge.'

'Leave a note for the service people telling them you've left, and asking them to take away what you've left. You'll want to drop the key off at the concierge's desk as well.'

Ten minutes later, feeling as though she were being marched towards an isolation cell, Sable reluctantly got into the front seat and kept her gaze fixed ahead when Kain eased his lean form in beside her and set the engine going.

When they drove out she realised the sky had clouded over, a heavy pall of grey pressing down on the city, barely skimming the volcanic hills that gave New Zealand's biggest city such a distinctive silhouette. In spite of the oppressive heat she shivered.

'Are you cold?'

He noticed too much. She could have sworn he hadn't taken his eyes off the road. 'No. This looks like cyclone weather.' Her voice sounded thin against the hum of the traffic.

'It's not a storm, just a tropical low. Rain's on the way with some wind, but it doesn't look as though it will be a problem.'

He drove well, guiding the big car through the central city traffic with fingers relaxed on the wheel.

After several minutes she realised they weren't heading for his apartment. 'Where are you taking me?' she demanded.

'I have a bach on the west coast. We need some time together alone.' Again his tone gave her no choice.

Cooped up in a bach with him... Baches, by definition, were small. She shivered again. The homestead, which had seemed so like a prison, suddenly appeared the much better option. At least there she'd have had some privacy.

'When are we coming back?' When he didn't answer straight away she said urgently, 'I have an event to organise, remember? Things need to be changed, and there's no way I can organise that from a bach on the west coast!'

Kain said, 'I'll give you a cell phone for emergencies, and we'll come back tomorrow night.'

Only one night there; her weight of apprehension lifted fractionally.

'And you will be, of course, perfectly safe.' He paused, then added smoothly, 'Or as safe as you want to be.'

'I hope I can trust you.' Her voice sounded raw instead of scathing, and too vulnerable.

'More—*much* more—than I can trust you.'

That hurt, but one glance at his iron-bound profile told her that further protestations of innocence would be futile. He had her tarred as a cheat on the make, and unless by some miracle she could prove her innocence he'd always believe it.

Hiding the debilitating hurt with tartness, she retorted, 'That remains to be seen.'

To her surprise he smiled, a movement of the beautiful mouth that sent a shivery little pleasure through her.

'How did you manage to work your way into a position of responsibility after the debacle of your first job?'

When she didn't answer he sent a probing glance sideways. 'Well?' An underlying note made the word a command.

Sable said curtly, 'With a lot of effort.'

Noting the purity of her profile and the reserved voice, Kain waited.

When the silence had stretched too long she added with palpable reluctance, 'I took a business degree at a polytech in western Auckland. But you probably already know that.'

He did, of course. More interesting was that she didn't tell him she'd worked an almost full-time job while she'd been taking that degree. Or that her course had been paid for by her father's insurance money.

Kain wondered what other schemes lay hidden in her past. At seventeen she'd been clever enough to get away with blackmail, aided by an employer who hadn't gone to the police presumably because of her link to his grandson.

Who'd been summarily dumped once she was off the hook.

And that could well have been Brent's fate if he hadn't stepped in.

Kain's mouth compressed. Rumour had it that she'd seduced the man as insurance against prosecution. Rumour could well be wrong, but it could also be right. Whatever, Derek Frensham seemed to have dropped off the face of the earth.

He noted the remoteness gathered around her like an icy cloak, and he was startled by a memory—of her mouth beneath his, soft and eager and infinitely seductive. His body tightened in an instinctive hunger. Despising himself for it, he banished the image to concentrate on driving.

Sable stared out at the rolling countryside, a thriving community of large country estates and working farms. Its mild climate, proximity to the coastline and Auckland, and above all its beauty made it a magnet for those rich enough to afford it, the well-manicured prosperity tempered only by a touch of raw New Zealand in the range of forest-covered hills that protected it from cold southerlies.

The oppressive silence in the car weighed her down. She was under attack, yet she had no way of protecting herself.

Kain slowed the car and turned down a gravel side road. That sensation of imminent danger intensified. Bracing herself, she said steadily, 'Look, you must know that this is a mad idea. You risk alienating Brent for ever—'

He cut her off without finesse. 'I know my cousin. Once he's accepted that we're in love—even temporarily—he'll wish us all the best and find someone else to play with.'

'Even if you're right—'

'I'm right.'

He eased the car around a tight corner, and the last golden rays of summer sun caught her full in the face. It gave her the excuse to shade her face from him while they headed for the west coast. The country got steeper and wilder as the road narrowed, and the light sharpened, became infused with an intensity that spoke of the sea.

Twin stone posts marked the end of the road—of civilisation, she thought with a foolish shudder. Just inside them the drive forked.

'The farm houses are along there,' Kain said with a brief gesture.

Was he trying to reassure her? From then on the drive dwindled into two gravelled wheel tracks with a strip of rank grass between them. They passed through a pine plantation, emerging onto more paddocks. It seemed a long time since she'd seen any sign of a house.

'Where is this?' she asked thinly.

Kain pulled in and stopped the car beneath an oak tree, one spread so wide it had probably been planted a century ago by an early settler. Its shade enclosed them in an umbrella of twilight.

Sable stiffened and turned her head away. The cattle in the nearest paddock—huge creamy things without horns—lifted their heads in mild interest, then resumed chewing the grass.

'What's the matter?' Kain asked abruptly, hard gaze on her profile.

Sable said on a rising note, 'What's the *matter*? Oh, nothing, except that I'm travelling who knows where with a man who's forced me into being here.' And only she appreciated the bitter irony of that! 'I don't even know where *here* is! Nobody knows where I am, or who I'm with, and you expect me to accept that without any qualms?'

His broad shoulders moved in a slight, careless shrug. 'Stop being so overdramatic. I don't plan to strangle you and throw you over a cliff.'

Grimly, enunciating each word through clenched teeth, she said, 'How do I know that?'

He reached into his pocket and tossed a cell phone at her. Her hands curved around it, warm from his body, a sleek, ultra-sophisticated thing. An odd sensation shot through her—part yearning for something that had never existed, part anger at his total lack of understanding.

And part irritation with herself because she didn't really fear for her safety—not her physical safety, anyway. What threatened her was something even more scary; although she was furious with him, deeper than that was a kind of hurt because he'd not only had her investigated, but he'd believed every sordid piece of gossip his private detective had brought to him.

Common sense told her not to be stupid. He didn't know her, and clearly he thought she posed a threat to Brent.

But some weak, romantic part of her mourned that she trusted him enough not to be a rapist and murderer, whereas he thought the very worst of her.

'Ring anyone you like and tell them where you are and who you're with,' he commanded.

She glanced across at him, met eyes the icy grey of a glacier, and shivered again. Giving into the inevitable, she silently entered a friend's number, mutely cursing when the answering machine delivered her friend's bubbly message.

'Hi, Libby, it's me,' she said brightly. 'It's five-thirty-five in the afternoon on Saturday, and we're off to the beach for the weekend at—'

She stopped, because she had no idea where they were going.

'Paritutu,' Kain said crisply, and took the phone from her fingers. 'Libby, Kain Gerard. We haven't met yet, but we will. I'm taking Sable to Paritutu on the west coast where I have a bach. If you need to contact her, here's the number.' He gave it then stowed the phone away again.

Somewhat reassured, she said brusquely, 'Thank you.' Then added impulsively, 'Why did you do that?'

He eyed her thoughtfully. 'What?'

'You had no need to leave Libby a message. She's going to be agog...'

'This is supposed to be a normal relationship between normal people,' he stated, his gaze level and intimidating. 'That means we meet each other's friends and family.'

'I have none,' she blurted. 'No family, anyway.'

And immediately wished she'd held the words back.

'Mine certainly make their presence felt,' he said dryly, putting the car into gear.

A thought struck her as they pulled out into the sunlight. Before she could reconsider her hasty words, she said, 'I hope you believed me when I told you that I wasn't going to sleep with you. All I'm prepared to give to this nasty little plan of yours is my physical presence.'

'I want more than that,' he said curtly.

'Then you can forget—'

'Not sex.' His tone was icy with contempt. 'But after this weekend we'll be living in my apartment and I'll want your complete co-operation in acting the part of my lover.'

Shaken by the uncompromising tone of his voice she turned her head away to stare unseeingly out of the side window.

Kain went on, 'So you'll stop flinching when I come near you, and make it obvious instead that you're in love with me—or at the very least madly attracted.' After a charged pause he went on with coolly delivered insolence, 'I'm sure you can do that.'

Heat stung her cheeks when the innuendo registered. Of course he knew she'd wanted him; her response to his kisses had been incandescent and terrifying. Rallying, she returned sweetly, 'Of course I can. Tell me, do you despise all women, or is it just me?'

'I despise dishonesty.' The hardness in his voice turned into cynicism as he added, 'On the other hand, I respect you for your enterprise.'

Lethally Sable purred, 'That's really, *really* big of you. Should I be grateful for that tiny instance of esteem?'

He surprised her by laughing, and to her chagrin it had real amusement in it. Of course it was easy to be in a good humour when you held all the good cards, she thought savagely.

And were ruthless enough to use blackmail to get whatever you wanted.

'Tell me about yourself,' he said, a lazy note of command reinforcing his position of power.

'Why? You've already been briefed on my character, apparently. You appear to believe you know everything about me—what more could I add?'

'I know the facts.' His tone reinforced his belief in them.

'If you think that more or less kidnapping me gives you the right to anything more than bare *supposed* facts, I'm afraid you're greatly mistaken.'

Where on earth had she produced the courage for that?

The knowledge she could hold her own—even temporarily—gave her the inducement to finish on a note of sarcasm, 'Since you've forced it onto me I'll endure this grubby charade, but I don't have to enjoy it, and I certainly don't have to spill everything about myself. After all, why should I? You've decided what sort of person I am and nothing I say will make you change your mind.'

He sent her a slanted glance. 'One thing I didn't learn about you is that you have a tongue like a viper,' he said appreciatively.

Before she could answer they crested a hill, and she breathed out a long, involuntary sigh.

'Welcome to Paritutu,' Kain said, slowing the car to a stop.

CHAPTER SIX

UNLIKE Kain's homestead on the other coast, Paritutu faced
a wilder, empty ocean; no islands, no vessels broke the
wide sweep of horizon, and waves marched onto the
crescent of burnished black sand with disciplined, military
precision, only to collapse into a white chaos of breakers.
These hills were higher than those that surrounded Totara
Bay, their gullies deeper, and the trees that clothed them
crouched against the slopes, sculpted by winds that had
made landfall after travelling across unsailed seas.

'What does Paritutu mean?' Sable asked, desperate to
break the silence.

'*Pari* is cliff, *tutu* erect. Sheer cliff.' Kain indicated the
southern headland, rockbound and frowning. 'The Maori
used to call the west coast the warrior coast because it's
stern and unforgiving and keeping yourself alive both on
shore and the sea requires constant vigilance.'

'And what did they call the east coast?'

'With its estuaries and islands and long sheltering pe-
ninsulas, its nurturing fisheries and beaches teeming with
seafood, what else but the feminine coast?' His tone turned
the query into a taunt.

'Typical male chauvinists,' Sable returned, hoping the

astringent words hid her embarrassing feeling of apprehensive excitement as he set the car in motion. The road twisted down towards a building she could just see amongst the pohutukawa and manuka bush.

It was humiliating to detest him with all the force of justified outrage, yet be aware of him so intensely it permeated every cell in her body, right to the tips of her toes.

What would she do if he decided to kiss her again? Slapping his face would merely make her look an idiot, because she doubted very much whether she'd be able to stay stiff and unresponsive. Even thinking about the open mastery of his kisses sent hot little shivers coursing through her, melting her apprehension into something appallingly close to anticipation.

Disgusted with herself, she concentrated on the scenery.

'Pre-European Maori certainly believed that men and women had different roles,' he agreed, 'as did Europeans of the same period. However, the Maori respected warlike women and those who gave good counsel as well as those who stuck to the traditional female roles.'

Just in time she stopped herself from saying, 'Big of them.' After all, the ancient Maori tribes with their rich culture weren't the focus of her anger.

Instead she asked, 'Do you have Maori ancestry?'

'Pacific Island. The original Gerard was French; he eloped with a paramount chief's daughter from Tahiti who just happened to be promised to another chief, so they had to flee to New Zealand. They settled at Totara Bay.'

No wonder he had hair as black as jet and those arrogantly aristocratic features—the mixture of Polynesian and French bloodlines had produced a superbly handsome man, she thought, trying hard to be snide instead of intrigued.

Fascinated in spite of herself, she said, 'Was that her portrait in the hall at Totara Bay?'

'Yes. Family legend has it that they fought like tigers, but after she died in childbirth he didn't marry again.'

'Who brought up the child?'

'His sister came out from France.'

He sounded surprised. Because she'd thought of the child? Sable conquered a fresh spurt of indignation.

'She was a nun,' he went on. 'Strict but loving, apparently; anyway, she stayed fifteen years before going back to her convent.'

He braked as a small flock of birds flew up from the road. Sable braced herself, then twisted to scan the road behind for small corpses. Relieved, she said, 'You missed them all.'

'Good,' he said, adding, 'The original house—a very primitive nikau whare—still exists behind the homestead at Totara Bay. If you're interested I'll show you when we go back.'

'Thank you,' she said primly.

'History interests you?'

Guardedly she admitted, 'Yes—especially personal history.' Perhaps because she knew nothing of her own; her father had never talked about his family or her mother's.

She glanced at him, the beautifully chiselled profile angular against the sombre coastal forest and remained silent until the bach came into view.

'Bach?' she asked incredulously. 'Baches are usually tiny!'

This house was not. Starkly modern, it didn't so much blend into the land and seascape as become part of it, its angles and stained wooden exterior a fitting foil for this wild area.

It couldn't have been a greater contrast to the Totara Bay homestead, all Victorian grace and charm.

'Did you build this?' she asked.

'Yes, to a design by Philip Angove.'

He said nothing more, but she thought the house and the place he'd chosen for it gave her an insight into his complex character that nothing else had done. The homestead had been his ancestors'—this was his own personal project, reflecting his tastes in a very individual way.

So why had he brought her *here*?

Still in silence they came to a stop outside the garage; he pressed a button and the door slid up to let them in, and down again behind them. Shut in the semi-darkness with him, Sable shivered.

'Here we are,' Kain said without any expression, and got out.

He hated her being here. Sable could feel it. This was the place of his heart, and he despised her.

How far was he prepared to go to protect his cousin?

What would it be like to have that powerful protective instinct directed at her?

Not ever going to happen, she thought, cold with something horribly close to desolation. She was the enemy, the intruder, the scoundrelly unwanted alien. Feeling more alone than she'd ever felt in her life, she resisted the temptation to stay stubbornly put; she wouldn't put it past him to leave her there.

Or to haul her out.

And that sent a honeyed, surreptitious shiver through her that warned her of her susceptibility. Gritting her teeth, she opened her door before he got there and swung her legs out, setting her chin at a defiant angle.

It was wasted. He stopped at the boot and took out her backpack and his own small bag. 'Ready?'

Sable's throat closed. The simple word seemed heavy with meaning, but she shied away from its implications. Swallowing, she said dryly, 'As ready as I'm likely to be.'

Inside, the house was every bit as dramatic as its exterior. Kain took her into a vast living room, its glass walls opening out onto a wide wooden deck that overlooked both the bush and the beach.

He dumped her backpack and his bag onto a sofa and went across to the doors, pushing them back to open the room to the wild scenery outside. A gust of fresh, salt-scented breeze swept into the room.

Silently Sable walked out onto the deck, inhaling air so fresh it filled her with a kind of wild exultation at the un-trammelled force of nature. Waves hammered onto the ebony sand, the clash of water and land setting free a haze of vapour that hung over the breakers like a veil.

From behind her Kain asked, 'How good a swimmer are you?'

'Excellent,' she said, adding, 'But I haven't swum in surf like this before.'

'It's different. Will you be afraid?'

She almost said, *Not of the waves*, but stopped the words before they could emerge.

Because she was *not* afraid of him.

If she was scared of anything it was her fierce response to him. It made her feel like someone else, a woman with no control over her feelings or actions—like her father when he'd been drunk.

And that was unbearable.

'Not afraid,' she said briskly, 'just cautious.'

He said, 'In that case you should be fine. I won't let you

drown, anyway.' He hefted her backpack and nodded towards a door. 'The bedrooms are through there. Mine is the first on the right. Come and choose one for yourself and I'll make up the bed.'

The thought of him making her bed was so charged with tantalising impact that her mind shied away from it. 'You'll do no such thing,' she returned, surprised that he didn't have menials to do the housework. 'You can tell me where the linen is and I'll do it myself.'

He lifted a brow. 'Becoming reconciled, Sable?'

How did he make her name sound like a prelude to seduction? She stiffened her spine and said with brittle poise, 'No.'

And if he thought she was going to choose the most distant bedroom from his he was mistaken; that would be too obvious. Right then she needed all the dignity she could summon. Of the four bedrooms she deliberately picked the second furthest away.

Once he'd left she pushed open the doors onto a deck and stepped out. The room had a magnificent sea view above the rounded domes of the huge pohutukawa trees that bordered this rocky end of the beach. She'd just put her backpack onto a chair when he returned, surprising her by carrying a pile of sheets and towels and pillowslips.

Casually he dropped them onto the big bed. 'The bathroom is through that door.' He indicated a door in the wall. 'It's an en suite, so you won't have to share with me.'

'You have no idea how overjoyed I am at that,' she said dulcetly, fighting back a vision of him in the shower, sleek with water glistening over that tanned skin…

His grin was sheer magic—charismatic, amused and infuriatingly knowing, as though he could read her mind. 'Oh, I'm sure you'd manage even that with admirable resourcefulness,' he drawled.

Cheeks hot, she returned, 'Thank you.' But when he jerked back the coverlet she blurted, 'I told you I'd make my own bed.' She stared at him, wishing he'd get out of the room, away from her, give her some respite from his overwhelming presence so that she could regroup her defences.

He inclined his head. 'Then I'll see you in twenty minutes or so.'

Somehow he managed to make it sound like an order. Resentfully she watched him leave the room, lowering her lashes to hide a gaze smouldering with a chaotic mixture of frustration and something treacherous she knew to be desire.

A glance at her watch told her she'd have time for a quick shower as well as unpacking and making her bed.

The unpacking bit took no time, although her clothes looked rather pathetic in the vast wardrobe. So? she thought staunchly, closing the door before taking the towels into the en suite, only to stop in the doorway with an involuntary gasp of appreciation. One wall of the bathroom was glass.

Awed and more than a little wary, she went across to it and looked out. It was completely private. No deck marred the view, and nor was it overlooked by any other part of the house. Her amazed gaze ranged from the empty sea to the headland. Sombre, magnificent, the rocky peak challenged the heaving restlessness of the wide expanse of ocean.

That inner wildness in Sable sang with a new song at the primal energy of the landscape, and the intense power in the never-ending conflict of earth and water.

Was this why Kain had built his house here?

'No,' she said out loud, turning away as she dismissed the idea.

That would mean that he and she had something in common, and she knew that wasn't so. Everything in this incredible day had taught her they shared nothing—not values, not beliefs, not aspirations. Nothing.

Beyond a certain physical lust, she reminded herself distastefully.

The bed made, she stripped her clothes and showered, keeping her head dry because she wasn't going to embarrass herself by appearing with dripping hair. However, as she put a few things away she discovered a hairdryer, still in its packet.

Who had bought it? Kain? She grinned, then sobered.

Actually, she could see him carrying off the purchase. His authority and confidence would deal with anything.

'Just as well I washed my hair this morning,' she said to her reflection, and tied the black length behind her head in a ponytail before getting into a pair of well-cut jeans that had been another good buy in her favourite second-hand shop. Because the air was still warm she topped them with a scoop-necked top in her favourite rose-red.

Then she hesitated, wondering if she should go out without any cosmetics as a sort of symbolic rejection. Too subtle?

Probably, she conceded.

Besides, for her cosmetics were more than an enhancement; she used them as a shield, a smooth, discreet armour to hide behind. But this time she applied the very minimum—a sheer veil of tinted foundation and lipstick the same colour as her top.

However, her final inspection brought her narrow brows together. Would he think she'd chosen that top deliberately because it showed a bit more skin? Did the slight hint of cleavage send the wrong message?

Another glance at her watch told her she didn't have

time to change; for some reason it was imperative she didn't take any longer than the twenty minutes he'd stated.

Ready for battle, she set her jaw and marched out.

The door into the sitting room was open. After a moment's foolish hesitation and a swift squaring of her shoulders she walked in.

'Right on time,' Kain said smoothly, looking up from a tray. 'Wine? Something stronger? Or non-alcoholic?'

'I'll have some wine, thank you,' she said, angry with her swift, combustible reaction at the sight of him in jeans that almost matched hers, a T-shirt revealing powerful shoulders and lean hips.

To hide the heavy pulse of her heart in her throat, she walked out onto a wide wooden deck. The glass doors somehow disappeared into the walls so that deck and room became one, and although it had almost the same magnificent, primeval view as her bedroom, it was sheltered from any breeze.

'I hope you like this,' he said from behind her. 'It's made from *viognier*, a grape that's new to New Zealand. I'm not sure we know how to deal with it yet, but this is a pleasant wine.'

'Thank you.' Mind racing, she took the glass. Small talk! She needed small talk.

After a cautious sip of the wine she let it slide down her throat before saying lightly, 'It's very pleasant. Did it come from your own vineyard?'

'One of them,' he told her.

She flushed, and Kain suddenly felt irritated by the casual thoughtlessness of his comment.

He'd been fortunate to grow up with a sound financial backing as well as firm parents with strong ideas on honesty and the virtues of hard work; how would he have ended up if he'd been deprived of real parental support and without any sort of moral values or standards?

Not that her father's alcoholism was any excuse for her blackmail attempt. Or for accepting a diamond ring from Brent, whom she must see as an easy mark.

And was he allowing himself to be seduced by her cool sultriness into a trap—that of seeking to redeem someone from their sins?

Hardly, he thought grimly, but moderated his tone when he told her, 'I own several.'

Sable sipped the delicate wine. Perhaps he was one of those enormously wealthy men who made a hobby of growing wine.

Somehow it was difficult to associate him with a hobby—the word seemed too relaxed, too ordinary for the man who'd almost casually forced her into a pretend love affair just to save his cousin from her supposed wiles. Beneath the superb good looks burned a dark fire, his ruthlessness backing up the brilliant intelligence that had taken him to the top of the business world in such a short time.

And she had to respect him for that. Reluctantly, she even respected him for his concern for Brent. Although, she thought vengefully, she'd bet he didn't take action in his business life on as little evidence as he had with her.

Her stomach hollowed out at the thought of the next few weeks.

'Wine-growing has to be a rich man's hobby,' she said tartly.

He shrugged. 'Not necessarily. I've met quite a few vineyard owners with nothing more than passion and hard work to back them up. And some are doing brilliantly—making boutique wines that stack up against anything the big players can produce.'

Interested in spite of herself, she said, 'Is that what your wines are? Boutique ones?'

'So far,' he told her, 'but my cellarmasters have ideas of expansion, so we'll see where we go. Apart from managing events, what do you see in your future?'

She lifted her glass in a silent toast. 'I hope there's some chance of staying out of trouble,' she said, wishing the flippant words back as soon as she'd said them.

A black brow was raised to sardonic effect. 'That seems a very limited ambition, and one easily attained. All you have to do is resist temptation.'

She gave a brief, jeering smile. 'So simple,' she agreed sweetly.

'While you're with me it had better be.'

His cold decisiveness sent a shiver through her, but she countered, 'There is a problem with that.'

After a charged moment he said icily, 'Which is?'

'You seem to be really good at jumping to conclusions.' She held his gaze without flinching. 'I do know when I'm outgunned—I'm not going to do anything stupid unless it's a social slip—but how do I know you're not going to come up with some other *supposed* sin from my past to force me into something else I don't want to do?'

'It depends on what else you've done. If you hadn't tried your hand at a spot of blackmail,' he pointed out with lethal contempt, 'I wouldn't have had the leverage. How did you manage to persuade Frensham to repay the money you extracted from his clients?'

Sable felt every muscle in her body freeze. So he knew. How? And when? Had he been testing her when he'd spoken only of forgery?

Almost certainly, she realised in bitter self-derision, and like an idiot she'd fallen into the trap, staying silent to

preserve what rags of pride she'd had left, and so reinforcing his belief she'd been the perpetrator.

'Leverage?' she asked with biting scorn. 'An interesting term—so much more *businesslike* than blackmail.'

His broad shoulders moved in a dismissive shrug. 'I can
understand that growing up in poverty, with a father who
drank himself into a stupor every night—'

'You know *nothing* about him,' she blazed, the stress of
the day suddenly overwhelming her. 'Yes, he was an alcoholic—although *he* faced facts and called himself a
drunkard—but he tried so hard to stop, to be the sort of
man he wanted to be.'

And each failure had driven him further into a darker
hell where he blamed himself for everything he couldn't
give her. Yet one thing she was certain of—he had loved
her as much as he was able to.

Furious with herself for losing control and aware that
Kain was watching her with something like pity, she took
a deep breath and held her head high, meeting his imper-
sonal, burnished gaze with pride and the pitifully few
scraps of dignity left to her. More temperately, she finished,
'And he didn't steal. He was the most honest man I've
known.'

'A pity you didn't follow his example,' Kain said evenly.

CHAPTER SEVEN

NUMBLY Sable said, 'I don't have to listen to you insult me.'

Kain's anger hit her like a freezing blast from the Pole. 'And I don't have to listen to any more lies.'

'Then don't raise the subject again.' She struggled to keep the hopelessness out of her tone. Why had it become so important that he believe her?

Apart from a natural dismay at being accused of something she hadn't done, there was something deeply personal about her reaction. Shocked and bewildered, she realised she desperately wanted Kain to understand instinctively that she was incapable of stealing money from the old man who'd offered her a job.

This hunger was different from the flashpoint of the sexual charge that shimmered between them; it was somehow more intimate, and consequently much more dangerous.

'I have no intention of doing so,' he said deliberately. 'But you need to know that if you give me reason I'll have no hesitation making good my threats.'

Stonily she said, 'Surely you can see that this isn't going to work? I dislike you every bit as much as you dislike me. Everyone—including Brent—will see we're just play-acting.'

'I don't think so,' he said softly, and when she stared at him he smiled and came towards her.

Sable swallowed to ease a dry mouth. 'What—no!'

But it was too late. He took the wine glass from her nerveless fingers and set it down on the table. The pale liquid shimmered and danced in the glass, and she realised that his hand couldn't have been quite steady.

A strange, reckless anticipation consumed her, robbing her of rational thought. Silently, helplessly, she looked up into a face honed by desire.

Yet when his mouth came down on hers she didn't move; he kissed her with such formidable passion that she caught fire. Her legs failed her, and he gave a kind of muted groan and brought her closer so that she could feel the power coiled in his lean body, the hunger that aroused him as potent and erotic as that untamed fever burning inside her.

When he lifted his head it was her turn to give a soft little sound, a plea for more.

Before she had time to feel ashamed of her open, naked need, he said in a taut, raw voice, 'What has *liking* to do with this, Sable?' and crushed the words into silence as he took her mouth again.

Without volition her arms curled around his neck, her breath sighing through her parted lips. This time he found the junction of her neck and shoulder and gently bit the acutely sensitive skin there.

A surge of sheer, animal pleasure from that light graze of his teeth sizzled through her like lightning, and in that flashpoint of desire she truly understood what *longing* meant. Then he nipped the lobe of her ear, his breath an erotic caress on her skin, and, panic-stricken, she thought that she was different now from her previous self, altered in some fundamental way by this man's expertise in lovemaking.

When he picked her up she didn't resist. Instead she buried her hot face in the angle of his neck, inhaling the faint body scent that had been sending such subliminal messages to her, and oddly—stupidly—basking in a sense of utter protection.

His arms tightened as he sat down with her on the huge leather sofa. At this evidence of his great strength a faint wisp of common sense struggled into life, only to vanish when he turned up her chin. Lost in the fathomless depths of his eyes, she felt her heart buck as he slid a finger beneath the neckline of her top.

'I've kissed all your lipstick off,' he said, that exciting roughness still in his voice. 'Why do you wear the stuff? Your lips are red and soft and delicious enough without it.'

Every sensory nerve quivering, she felt his finger move a little further beneath the soft material of her top. When he'd carried her—or perhaps when he'd sat down on the sofa, she was in no state to remember—the hem of her shirt had ridden up, and his other hand now rested on her bare skin, warm and strong and compelling.

'I like the colour,' she said inanely, then flushed, because he laughed quietly, his eyes narrowed and glittering.

Lord, was that *her* voice—a betraying mixture of huskiness and a breathy hesitance she'd never heard before?

He kissed her again, and when he let her surface from the mists of sensuality he was stroking the upper part of her breast, setting off more fires through her body with each slow caress.

Sable fought the need to squirm against him, but failed. His response was instantaneous and abrupt; he pulled her further into his lap so that the rigid length of his penis pressed against her. His free hand swooped up under her shirt, and cupped her other aching, pleading breast.

Kain looked down at her. 'We seem to be stretching the fabric of this pretty thing. Would you be more comfortable if I took it off?'

He waited for her response, aware that he was giving her an out. Would she take it? Her slumbrous, dark eyes were half-hidden by heavy lashes, and her cheeks were warmed by a delectable soft glow, her mouth sensuously pouting.

However, he wanted no angry denunciations later, no accusations of forcible seduction. Sexy and utterly desirable as she was, he didn't trust her an inch. She was going to have to give her assent every step of the way.

Every muscle in his body clenched with an aching hunger. Damn, but he wanted her!

'Sable?' he asked again, when she said nothing.

Lifting drowsy lashes, she smiled. 'T-shirts *are* inclined to stretch badly,' she said in that smoky voice.

Clever, he thought—neither a yes or a no. Paradoxically her quick mind inflamed the desire that had been building in him ever since he'd first laid eyes on her.

But he wasn't going to let her get away with it. 'Answer me, Sable.'

White teeth closed a second on her tender lower lip. Then, as colour swept across her magnificent cheekbones, she murmured, 'It has to be a yes, I suppose.'

And that, he decided, was as close to a straight answer as he was likely to get from her. Resisting a surge of hunger so acute it damned near unmanned him, he waited for her to take the pretty ruby-coloured thing off.

When the only movement she made was to turn her face into his throat again, he prompted, 'Sit up, then.'

Languorously she obeyed, her slender body causing mayhem in his every cell when she eased the shirt over her head.

Kain fought back a guttural exclamation and the inclination to clench his hands. God, the last thing he wanted to do was mark her satiny skin! She was sleek and sinuous, and that blush had travelled upwards from the edge of the delicate scraps of silk that protected her high breasts.

Surely she wasn't as inexperienced as that enchanting colour made her seem?

The primitive desire to be the man who initiated her into the delights of passion caught him by surprise; even as he tried to control it, he wondered at the astonishing pleasure gripping him.

But Sable was no virgin.

Another wave of heat burned through Sable as she felt the impact of Kain's scrutiny right through to her heart's core. Fire licked through her veins—languorous, smouldering, an erotic summons. Although she'd idolised Derek, basking foolishly in the belief that his caresses meant he loved her, he'd never made her feel like this—so wild, so free, so ardently abandoned.

Kain said quietly, 'You are beautiful.'

A faint, wistful smile curled her lips. Derek had told her often enough that she was beautiful, but it had been all false.

Just as she'd been unwittingly lying when she'd told him she'd loved him; loneliness had driven her into his bed, and a childish hunger for love and protection.

She wouldn't make that mistake again.

At least Kain made no false promises, no pretence. He disliked her, but his passion was honest and real, and she wanted it so much…

A wave of aching anticipation broke over her, washing away her reservations and her cowardly fears. 'What's sauce for the goose…' she said huskily. 'Why don't *you* take off your shirt?'

Eyes gleaming, he let her go and leaned back against the sofa with arms outspread. 'Why don't you take it off?' he challenged.

Her fingers shook as she reached for the hem of his shirt and began to lift it. Avoiding his gaze, she stifled the itch to explore the tanned skin revealed as she eased up the warm fabric. He raised his arms and bent his black head forward; she slid the shirt over it and let it drop to join hers on the floor.

And then she halted, mind and emotions in turmoil, not knowing what to do next.

His chest expanded in a quiet laugh. He must have discerned her total lack of confidence, because he took her hand and held it against his heart.

'What do you feel?' he asked.

The heavy throb beat against her palm. 'Your life,' she said almost inaudibly, excited all over again at the realisation that she was doing this to him.

She bent her head and kissed the spot, letting her lips linger over his skin, then with delicate swiftness licking it. His taste filled her mouth—salty, a little musky, delicious.

Then she gasped as her bra fell away, discarded like their shirts. He lifted her and kissed her between her breasts, and she felt her heart go crazy when his lips lingered.

'And I can feel yours,' he said thickly. 'You taste like some exotic aphrodisiac.'

He lowered her, his arms coming around her as he positioned her so that his mouth could reach the peak of one breast.

Sable held her breath, eyes closing in voluptuous pleasure at the gentle tug of his lips. She clutched him, her fingers slipping helplessly across the hot sleekness of his skin while raw excitement pulsed through her.

'Kain,' she whispered, barely able to articulate.

He lifted his head. 'Yes.'

Just one word; a challenge?

No, she thought dazedly, the time for challenge was past; he'd made his answer a claim, decisive and masterful, a claim she accepted. Their eyes met and clashed—hers dark and questioning, his half-closed, fiercely demanding. She fought a brief, desperate battle for common sense, then with a rashness she'd never felt before, flung it away.

For tonight…

'Last chance, Sable,' he said between his teeth.

'Yes,' she said, a smile trembling on her mouth.

He held her gaze to the point of discomfort before surprising her with a long, almost tender kiss that turned abruptly fierce when he began to unfasten her jeans, pushing them down until she lay in his lap clad only in one brief garment.

Wordlessly, mouth open to the possession of his, she shuddered erotically at the touch of his fingers against her skin. Sensation roared through her—torrid, headstrong. He kissed her other breast before making it his own.

But when he'd reduced her to a shivering excitement he said against her skin, 'Your turn, Sable.'

She looked blankly at him.

An odd smile quirked his mouth. He took her hand and put it on the front of his jeans. Colour blossomed across her face as she fumbled with the zip, wishing there was some easy way of doing this.

He waited until she'd dealt with the fastening, then ran his fingers through her hair, loosening it from the tie and letting it fall around her shoulders.

'Like silk,' he said, his voice deep and harsh, and twisted away to shuck off his last clothes.

Her breath stopped in her throat. He was glorious, a bronze god, she thought with aching hunger, the swift coil and flexing of his muscles beneath the skin erotic in itself, the shadow of hair across his chest arrowing suggestively down.

And he was *big*...

He said, 'I need to get protection.'

'No, it's all right.' She met his narrowed eyes defiantly. 'There are other reasons for taking contraceptive pills than to prevent babies.'

He scanned her face, then said, 'Nevertheless, just to make sure—'

Chilled, she watched him straighten, then squeaked when he stooped and picked her up, his arms closing around her with intensely stimulating strength. 'Besides,' he said, heading towards the door, 'we'll be more comfortable on a bed. Being oversize is a disadvantage sometimes.'

'You're not oversize,' she protested, her voice soft and smoky. She ran a finger along his shoulder, watching from beneath half-lowered lashes as the muscles tightened. 'You're tall and...' Her voice died away.

Perfect.

'And?' he prompted with a glint in his eye.

Hastily she said the first thing that came to mind. 'Very masculine.'

He shouldered through a door and strode across the room. *His* room, she realised after he'd put her down on a huge bed.

Well, of course—that's where he'd keep his contraceptives. Suddenly shy, she closed her eyes.

How many other women had he made love to in this great bed, in this room, shadowy now with approaching twilight?

The question pierced her, but when he came down beside her and she was again enfolded in his warmth, his special, subtle scent teasing her nostrils, his mouth on hers again, all thoughts fled and she was once more prisoner of her need.

Somehow he managed to remove her last garment with no fuss.

She braced herself for his body on top, startled when he settled in beside her and slid his hand down to the over-sensitive, eager juncture of her legs. It took all of her will-power not to arch against the pressure, inviting a deeper, harder touch, an even more intimate invasion.

In an edged voice he said, 'Look at me, Sable.'

A frown pulled her brows together and she kept her eyes firmly shut. She felt his kisses on her eyelids, fleeting and light, but his voice held a ring of command when he said, 'Open your eyes.'

'Why?' she croaked.

'Because I want you to see me.'

Dazed, almost frantic with longing and apprehension, she managed to lift her lashes enough to see him. He was looking down at her, and when she returned that look he smiled and said, 'Sable.'

'Kain,' she replied without volition.

He kissed her again, and as her lashes drifted down she felt the movement of his fingers into her, and her whole body convulsed against his experienced, dangerously ad-dictive caress.

It had never happened to her before, that desperate sur-render to desire, and as the wonderful waves faded into a lazy, sated pleasure, she was stunned.

She was even more surprised when he held her against him for long moments before saying with a hint of irony, 'Women have it over men there. Now, let's see how we go.'

Sable expected him to take his own satisfaction, and it would all be over. Instead he began again, his lingering caresses and deep, deep kisses reawakening her appetite so that she began to tense and arch with the need he aroused.

And finally, when she was incoherent with hunger, he moved over her and into her, a slow, purposeful entry that made her moan. By then she was gripping his shoulders, feeling them wet beneath her fingers, the muscles knotting as he controlled his hunger.

With formidable patience Kain stoked their passion, each thrust taking her closer and closer to something— some tumultuous experience—something she'd never experienced, not even before in his arms when she'd thought she'd reached a peak...

She could hear herself sobbing his name and then pleading for an ending she couldn't—quite—reach, the frantic words tumbling through her brain with no echo.

Kain said something in a low, guttural voice and began to move faster, forcing her further and further upwards, until the torrents of ecstasy overwhelmed her in a savagely rapturous fulfilment. Almost immediately Kain joined her, a harsh groan wrenched from him before he collapsed onto her.

Eventually he said, 'I'm crushing you.'

'No.' Unconsciously she tightened her arms around his back.

But he turned onto the bed beside her, arms still locked around her. Sable realised that she was crying—not great huge gulps but slow tears that burned her eyes. Blinking ferociously, she concentrated on the rise and fall of his breathing against her...

Later she realised she must have slipped into sleep,

because when she woke it was to find herself being carried again.

'What—?' she said, dazed and wondering where she was.

'It's all right. I'm just taking you to your own bed.'

He sounded distant, as though his thoughts were elsewhere. The sting of rejection was acutely painful, but salutary. Far better to wake up alone tomorrow morning than be forced to face him after spending the night with him—a much more intimate thing than the transient sharing of their bodies, however ecstatic that had been.

But once in her own bed she couldn't sleep. Covered only by a sheet as the dull roar of the surf on the beach pounded through the room, she tried to find some sense in her tumbling thoughts and emotions.

Making love with Kain had been nothing like the hurried, unsatisfactory experiences she'd shared with Derek: a few kisses, a quick fumble and grope, then penetration, all over in a few minutes, leaving her embarrassed and wondering why on earth people made all that fuss over such a mundane thing.

At first Kain had been gentle, almost tender, as though he'd understood that this was all very new. He'd made her feel—cherished...

And then he'd made her feel wild and abandoned and desperate, so hungry for the sensations he roused in her that she'd lost all reserve. Her skin heated as she recalled her complete surrender to the smell and feel and taste of him, and then the powerful loss of herself in passion.

It had been heart-shaking, like a rebirth.

Oh, for heaven's sake, she scoffed silently—all you did was make love. People do it all the time; it doesn't really mean anything if it's done without emotion.

And Kain certainly didn't feel anything but contempt

for her. For him it had probably been a cynical exercise in domination. Yes, he'd made sure she reached her peak first, waiting to take his own satisfaction until she convulsed in his arms, but Kain was cleverer than Derek and far more ruthless. Perhaps he wanted her to fall a little bit in love with him so that she'd be more amenable.

Or so she'd convince Brent that any hopes he had were doomed?

Yes, that made bitter sense.

Hot and restless, she twisted between the sheets, trying to evade her thoughts and the clamour deep in her body.

And yet she couldn't forget Kain's unexpected consideration, the way he'd held her after she'd shattered in his arms, the smoothing of her tangled hair back from her brow…

God, she'd go mad. Sable turned onto her back and stared at the unseen ceiling. Perhaps the strange wildness in her blood had come from this primeval place. No, that was a stupid, overdramatic notion, trying to blame her behaviour on the landscape!

Driven by restlessness, she got out of bed, acutely aware of sundry pleasant aches in her body, and walked across to the wall of glass, holding the curtains back so she could see the white lines of breakers in their ceaseless formations. No moon lit the sky, almost bare of clouds now although a dark line just above the horizon to the north indicated that more were on the way. Endless stars dazzled against the black sky, lending earth and sea a luminous sheen.

A breeze ruffled the leaves of the great trees that sheltered the house, turning them so the felted undersides shimmered in silver flecks against their sombre darkness.

She stayed there a while, searching for some peace, some resolution, and finding nothing but more questions to ask, until she saw a movement on the beach.

Kain, she knew instantly, her heart quickening. She narrowed her eyes, hungrily picking out the straight carriage, the lithe gait, the powerful silhouette of his big body against the star-gleam on the sea.

So he couldn't sleep either.

Hastily she let the curtain fall and crept back to her bed, waiting for him to come into the house. At last she heard slight sounds, and as though his mere presence fulfilled some deep-seated primal need she fell asleep.

But when she woke the next morning she knew that she couldn't afford to allow any more lovemaking. It was far too dangerous.

She got into a pair of white jeans and a cotton shirt with sleeves down to her wrists because the air had cooled since the previous day.

No, she admitted, because she felt more in control with as much skin covered as possible. After making the bed and fussing around—putting off the moment as long as possible—she took a long controlled breath and went out of the room.

It didn't help when she found the clothes she'd worn the night before neatly folded in a heap outside her bedroom door. Flushing, she picked them up and took them into her room, standing with them in her hands as she looked blankly around.

She was not going to put them out to be washed! After a moment's blankness she grabbed a plastic bag and stuffed them into it.

She stood for a minute or so with her hands clenched at her sides, taking more even breaths, before she regained enough composure to walk out and face Kain.

CHAPTER EIGHT

THE seductive scent of bacon greeted Sable when she opened the door into the huge room that served as both living and dining room. Until then she hadn't realised that she'd been swept into Kain's arms before dinner, but in an instant she was ravenously hungry.

Kain turned as she entered. Handsome features hard-honed in the cloudy morning light, his mouth a straight slash and pale eyes uncomfortably piercing, he said from behind the breakfast bar, 'Good morning. I hope you like bacon and eggs.'

'Very much, thank you.' Yes, her voice was fine—level, a little reserved, far removed from the breathless, broken tones that had so startled her the previous night. Intrigued and wary, she watched him moving with complete confidence around the kitchen.

'Good. Would you rather eat in here or on the deck?'

'The deck,' she told him without hesitation. She needed space. 'Tell me where stuff is and I'll set the table.'

Thank heavens for the ordinary chores of daily life, and the necessary small talk that accompanied them and filled up charged silences!

By the time she'd set two places, asked him where the

salt and pepper were kept, chosen three vibrantly gold hibiscus flowers from the bush at the end of the deck, and used the juicer to produce a concoction of passionfruit, feijoa and pineapple juice, she'd regained some composure.

Except for the moments when her memory taunted her with flashbacks of what she'd felt the previous night, churning up wild emotions and sensations she wished she could banish.

It was no solace that he was completely self-possessed, but no doubt he'd done this hundreds of times before. After all, he'd had several serious relationships, so breakfasting with a woman would be no novelty.

Whereas she'd never even spent the night with a man; Derek had always left after they'd made love.

Kain said, 'You must be starving.'

'I am hungry,' she admitted.

He was a good cook. The bacon was perfect, the poached eggs round and unbroken, grilled tomatoes just at the right stage of squishiness.

'Is that why you're looking so harried?' he enquired smoothly as he sat down opposite her.

Her appetite fled. 'I simply don't know the protocol involved after sleeping with a man who not only actively dislikes me but suspects me of being a criminal.' She bit out the final words. 'Forgive me if I seem clumsy and socially inept.'

That inquisitorial brow lifted. 'Second thoughts, Sable?'

And third and fourth and fifth ones. 'I can't help thinking that last night was one of the more stupid things I've done in my life.'

'And you've done some very foolish things.' His tone

was judicial. 'One of them was not denying that your supposed crime was fraud.'

'Stupid of me,' she said, hiding a stab of pain with a tight smile. 'But forcing me into this whole situation makes you just as evil as you think I am.'

'I did not blackmail you into my bed.'

Every nerve in her body jerked into full flight-or-fight response. He'd spoken quietly, but his hooded, dangerous look told her she'd hit home with her accusation.

Reluctantly she said, 'Agreed.'

'And if you're preparing to tell me that you don't want to make love again, that's a decision I'd already made,' he told her, his expression unyielding. 'Toast?'

'Thank you.' Saved by the ordinary conventions of life again. But a residual crackle of tension in the atmosphere warned her not to push things. She said inanely, 'This is delicious. Where did you learn to cook?'

'My aunt felt that every man should learn to cook a roast dinner and a full breakfast as well as make an excellent salad.'

'Wise woman.' Would that be Brent's mother? But Brent seemed to live on hamburgers with an occasional foray into orgies of bananas.

Kain gave a hard smile. 'And as I lived with her and Brent after my parents were killed, she had the opportunity to make sure I learned to do it all to her exacting standards.'

Startled, she looked up. 'I see.' No doubt that was why he felt so protective towards his cousin, more like a big brother.

His face didn't give anything away. 'A car crash,' he said succinctly, guessing the question she didn't like to ask.

Horrified, she blurted, 'Were you there?'

'In the back seat—with a seat belt on, so I came through it without anything more than scratches. They were arguing and my mother was making one of her grand gestures—she accidentally hit the steering wheel with her outflung hand. The car careered onto the other side of the road and over the edge.'

Kain stopped abruptly, wondering how the *hell* that had emerged. He'd never told anyone—not his aunt, nor the investigators who'd tried to find out what had caused the crash.

Yet here he was spilling his guts to a woman he had every reason to dislike and distrust. And although he'd decided during a mostly sleepless night that he wasn't going to make love to her again, for some unusual—and suspicious—reason he'd had to control a violent surge of anger when it had become obvious she'd arrived at the same decision.

Her calm acceptance should have reinforced his distrust. So it was ironic that all he could recall was her fiery passion, the sweet recklessness of her complete surrender.

It was impossible to read her thoughts; her provocative face hid every emotion. Grimly he focused on the diamond ring she'd pocketed from Brent even though she'd told his cousin she wasn't in love with him. And then there was her cold-hearted betrayal of an old man who'd given her a job when no one else would.

If that had really happened…

The query slid into his mind seductively. His head of security hadn't been able to track Derek Frensham down. But there was the woman who'd been blackmailed—a Gwenneth Popham. She'd left the district soon after and she'd been old then, so she was probably dead, but he'd ordered his man to keep digging.

Quietly, her voice sympathetic, she said, 'That must be a dreadful last memory to have of your parents.'

Dismissing the momentary flash of weakness that had him wanting to prove her innocent, he shrugged. 'I have plenty of happy ones. My mother had a quick temper, but she would have died for my father and me.'

'I never knew my mother.' She put down her knife and fork and looked past him towards the dunes behind the beach. In a remote little voice she said, 'Apparently the pregnancy was a bad mistake; she didn't want to have me. My father talked her into keeping me, but as soon as I was born she left.'

Kain felt an unwanted tug of sympathy. If that was true it might explain a lot.

He hadn't planned on bedding her quite so soon. Not that it would make any difference; she'd clearly been ready, and making love had done exactly what he wanted—made her acutely aware of him. When Brent returned he was going to be in no doubt that Kain and Sable were lovers.

His cousin would be angry, perhaps even grieve for a while, but eventually he'd realise that he'd got off lightly. Especially when he realised that Sable had probably planned to bleed him dry before she left.

She said now, 'But you don't miss what you've never had. I'm so sorry about your parents.'

Her dark eyes were warmly sympathetic, her tone quiet and sincere.

'It happened a long time ago.' He knew he sounded brusque, but even now the memory of his mother's scream as they'd hurtled over the bank had the power to lift the hair on the back of his neck.

The sudden loud irruption of an engine turned both their heads. 'What the hell?' Kain said lethally, and came to his feet in a swift, explosive movement.

The vehicle roared on past the house and down to the beach—a farm quad bike, Sable saw as she scrambled up too, with three teenaged boys perched on it, their faces alight with pleasure.

'Who are they?' she asked.

'Nobody who should be here.' He strode inside and when she followed him she heard him say into the telephone, '…would never give permission for quads to be used on the beach or in the dunes.' He paused to listen to whoever was on the other end, then said curtly, 'No, I'll go down.'

He put the telephone down and said to Sable, 'Stay here.'

Torn, she hesitated, then firmed her mouth. 'I'll come with you.'

'I don't need you,' he said curtly.

There came a grinding sound, a yell quite different from the jubilant ones of a few seconds previously, and then silence as the engine sputtered out.

Kain said something she was glad she didn't quite hear, then picked up the phone again, speed-dialled and barked, 'They've crashed the quad. Get Vanessa down here fast,' into it before slamming it down. Eyes hard he looked at Sable. 'Come on—but not if you're going to be useless. There could be blood.'

There was. He moved very fast for a big man, getting there ahead of Sable, who panted to a stop as she took in two sprawled bodies, both ominously still. One had been flung free, but the other was trapped underneath the vehicle. The third youth was bending over the upturned quad, trying to haul it off his friend. He looked up as they ran towards them, his face white and fearful.

'I can't move it,' he said in a thin, high voice, and choked back a sob.

Kain ordered, 'Sable, see to the kid on the ground. Check his breathing and then stop the bleeding.'

She dropped to her knees beside the boy—fifteen or sixteen, she guessed, and he was alive, thank God, but he was unconscious and his stertorous breathing worried her almost as much as the ugly wound to his thigh that was pumping out blood in great jets.

For a moment she thought she might faint. Overcoming nausea and dizziness by sheer willpower, she looked around for something—anything—to staunch the arterial flow, then remembered the instructions she'd received at her high school first-aid course and pressed her fingers above the wound, hoping that would stop that ominous spurting.

But the blood still surged out. Anxiously she scanned his face. Was he getting paler? He'd lost enough blood for this to be a real emergency.

Tourniquets were dangerous, but it looked as though this was going to need one. First though she'd try straight pressure to the wound. Praying she was doing the right thing, she tore off her shirt, wadded it into a pad and pressed it over the jagged tear in his skin.

Within seconds it was obvious it wasn't going to work; her stomach heaved as blood kept welling remorselessly through the material.

She gritted her teeth and thanked the embarrassment that had made her wear something with long sleeves. Hands shaking, she twisted the sleeve around his thigh above the wound, cursing steadily and silently when the wet material slipped and knotted, refusing to tie. About the only thing she could remember was that the knot had to be one she could release.

Afterwards she thought she'd held her breath until the

blood flow began to ease. 'Oh, thank God,' she sighed, and glanced over her shoulder.

Kain was hauling the quad off the other boy, the muscles beneath his T-shirt bulging with the effort it took.

'Be careful,' she whispered, and gasped when he finally got it off.

Kain dropped to his knees and examined the youth beneath it, his frown deepening. The third boy stood to one side, his chest heaving with exertion, his face anguished.

Kain reached into his trouser pocket and started talking crisply into his cell phone. A few seconds later he snapped it shut, looked at her, and came across in two strides, ripping off his shirt as he came and throwing it at her.

'Put it on,' he ordered. 'How is he?'

'I don't know, but he needs more than simple first aid,' she told him, struggling into the shirt. A faint musky fragrance floated around her, and for a moment the stench of blood receded; oddly comforted, she turned back to the boy on the ground.

Worriedly she said, 'I think he might have a fracture, and he was losing blood awfully fast. I've put a tourniquet on it, but I have no idea how long it's safe to leave it.'

Dimly she heard the high pitch of her voice and drew a ragged breath, cutting the words short. The boy on the ground probably couldn't hear her, but babbling like an idiot was stupid and counterproductive. Forcing herself to speak steadily, she ended, 'But we can deal with it. How is the other boy?'

'The quad is off him.' Kain too was being circumspect. 'My farm manager is on his way with his wife, who's a registered nurse and I've just called the rescue chopper. They said not to move either of them.'

Her patient was stirring, opening eyes as round and innocently cornflower-blue as a child. 'Mum?' he whispered, then frowned and his lashes fluttered down.

'What's his name?' Sable asked of the other boy who'd followed Kain across and was standing awkwardly watching.

'Nigel, but we call him Corky,' he said, his voice cracking.

'Corky.' She leaned across the boy, projecting complete confidence into her voice. 'Corky, you're going to be all right.'

He frowned again and groaned. 'Hurts,' he muttered, turning his head restlessly.

'You're going to be all right,' Sable said, projecting confidence into her voice. 'Just hang on, Corky. You're going to be fine, but we have to wait for the helicopter. It won't be long now.'

She glanced over; Kain had left her to go back to the boy he'd rescued, and something about the set of his broad, bronzed shoulders made her shiver. The third youth shifted from foot to foot uncertainly, looking up with an expression of deep relief when a four-wheel drive came tearing down the hill.

It carried the farm manager and his wife, who took over with brisk competence. From snatches of overheard conversation Sable discovered that the two hurt boys were brothers, staying on the farm with the one who was hovering miserably by. His pale, shocked parents soon arrived in another vehicle.

Corky seemed to be drifting in and out of consciousness, but whenever she stopped talking he frowned again and tried to turn his head towards her. Sable stayed with him, exhorting him to hang on, telling him that the chopper was coming soon, that all he had to do was keep going.

Her voice was strained by the time the sound of the helicopter coming low and fast over the hills brought a sharp sigh of relief. After that it was a controlled bustle until both boys were loaded into the chopper. Accompanying them was the woman they were staying with; her husband had already rung their parents who were heading towards the hospital.

The chopper took off in a haze of sand and noise. Sable stood limply by, watching it, acutely conscious of Kain's arm across her shoulders. She relaxed, letting herself sag against him.

'You did well,' his farm manager's wife told her.

'Are they going to be all right?'

The older woman frowned. 'I don't know. Young Corky is probably OK, but Sandy…'

The sound of another engine turned all their heads. 'The police,' Kain said crisply.

The policeman asked questions and took photographs of the scene, asked Sable and Kain more questions, and finally took his departure.

Sable said, 'I think I'd like some coffee.'

'Me too.' Kain stooped to pick up her gory shirt. 'Will you be able to save this?'

'I doubt it,' she said, shuddering.

He caught her hand in his. 'Come on, let's go.'

Her knees felt distinctly wobbly, and she was grateful for his strength and warmth as they walked back up to the house. They were almost there when she said, 'Do *you* think they'll make it?'

'Corky should, even though he's badly shocked,' he said curtly. 'The other boy's in a worse state.'

She shivered; the helicopter staff had been so careful, loading both boys onto stretchers specially constructed for spinal injuries.

It must have been horrible for Kain; he'd seen his parents die, and then to deal with this…

Clearly he didn't want to discuss it. In silence they walked up to the house and the cold remains of breakfast. He surveyed them with distaste. 'I'll make coffee,' he said, 'and cook something else.'

'I'm not hungry,' she said swiftly.

'Nevertheless I'll make toast. You're a bit shocked and you need something. We'll both have sugar in our coffee too.'

Stomach churning, she pulled a face but said, 'Toast will be fine, thank you.'

'I take back what I said about blood,' he said unexpectedly. 'You coped very well. I'm sorry about your shirt.'

'It doesn't matter,' she said dismissively, then added on a worried sigh, 'I just hope I helped and didn't make things worse. I know tourniquets aren't a good thing except in the direst emergencies but I couldn't stop the bleeding any other way…'

He looked down at her and without volition she walked into the arms that opened and then closed around her. He hugged her for a long moment, letting her bask in his human warmth and strength.

Deep inside her, some inner tension eased a little.

Perhaps, she thought as she recalled the two boys lying so still on the sand, he was taking comfort from her closeness too. The accident *must* have brought back his parents' deaths, with who-knew-what hideous memories.

Eventually he said, 'You did well—you deserve the credit for saving young Corky's life.'

'Rubbish,' she said into his chest. 'If I hadn't been there you'd have had the other boy making a tourniquet and applying it.'

'We were busy getting the quad off. Corky would have bled out before we got to him.'

She shivered. 'How can we find out whether or not they make it?'

'I'll ring Geoff—the manager—tonight. He'll have the latest details.' He let her go and in a rigid, aloof voice said, 'Right, let's get coffee and toast going.'

Back to square one, she thought, repressing a shiver.

It was too easy to let herself forget that Kain was cold-bloodedly using her, and the magical comfort of his arms nothing more than a chimera.

She didn't entirely blame him for believing she'd blackmailed Mr Frensham's clients. Derek had been cunning, and because the case had never come to court there was no evidence to exonerate her. Sometimes at night she still woke terrified, returned by her dreams to the days when she'd been sure she'd go to prison.

When the truth came out she'd been so relieved she'd just wanted to leave it all behind her. Now she wished she could fling proof of her innocence in Kain's face, force him to apologise.

And that, she realised as they worked together to make the coffee and toast, was a really scary warning sign. Kain's good opinion of her didn't—*shouldn't*—matter. The last thing she needed in her life right now was to fall in love with Kain Gerard.

Hadn't she learned her lesson? She'd been shattered to find out that Derek had used her to gain access to his grandfather's files. Not just that, either; he'd quite deliberately set her up. She'd thought she was heartbroken, and since then she'd deliberately kept away from all emotional entanglements.

But it hadn't been a broken heart she'd suffered—more,

she thought now, humiliation because Derek's betrayal had stripped away her fragile confidence as a woman.

Well, she'd fought back, but falling in love with Kain would be a disaster, with heartbreak its inevitable result.

All right, she told herself as she gulped some coffee, so no falling in love.

'How are you feeling?' Turning her to face him, he scrutinised her. 'You're too pale.'

Hair lifting on the back of her neck, she looked up. 'I'm fine, thank you. I just needed some caffeine.'

He held her eyes for a moment, then let her go to pick up the newspaper, but she had the uncomfortable feeling that those ice-coloured eyes had discerned her thoughts.

For the rest of the day Kain was solicitous but reserved. They walked along the beach—away from the scene of the accident—and he told her about the revegetating of the dunes with a native plant.

After lunch he closeted himself in a study while she read out on the deck. When the sun began stroking her face with golden light she got up and eased herself into a hammock slung from a huge pohutukawa branch. It looked like being a fantastic summer, she thought sleepily, and somehow managed to doze off.

When Kain came out, he frowned as he looked around. Some small part of him relaxed when he saw her gracefully sleeping in the hammock. His gut tightened. Damn, he thought with cold disgust, last night should have sated him, but he still wanted her!

Right now, in the hammock.

Making love to her had whetted his lust, not satisfied it. He could feel the hunger, a feral, consuming urge to slide his hand beneath the shirt that had rucked up, giving him a glimpse of the white skin above her waist.

He'd just finished talking to the boys' mother, who'd rung to thank him for his help. 'Sandy's still unconscious, but Nigel came to, and he—he said an angel told him to hang on, not to give up,' she'd told him, her voice thickened with tears. 'I'd like to speak to her, thank her.'

'I'm afraid she's not available,' Kain said, making up his mind instantly. No way was he going to introduce Sable to Corky's—Nigel's—mother. Sable had done her best for the boy, but that didn't mean that she was safe to introduce to a woman who felt so beholden to her.

So he said smoothly, 'I'll convey your thanks to her.'

'She saved his life—and I don't mean putting the tourniquet on his leg and knowing what to do with it, although of course that helped.' She dragged in a shuddering breath. 'Nigel said all he wanted to do was go to sleep but she kept talking to him, and he really wanted to be able to open his eyes and see if she was as beautiful as she sounded.'

Her voice had risen slightly, almost as though she was asking a question.

He'd said formally, 'Mrs McCorkindale, I'll tell her that you thank her. Do keep me in touch with your son's progress, won't you?'

Now, looking across at Sable's relaxed face, he wondered if he was being foolishly cautious.

But dealing well with an emergency was no indication of high moral standards, he thought grimly.

An angel, Corky had called her. Oh, he thought cynically, the innocence of the young...

He started down the steps to the hammock. Sable must have sensed his arrival because she woke, lashes fluttering up to reveal those dark eyes, deep enough to drown in. She smiled, and breathed his name in a husky, yearning cadence, holding out her arms to him as though he was all she'd ever wanted.

Kain's blood surged through him; he bent, then the sound of an engine penetrated the fog of desire in his brain. Cursing the interruption, he straightened and turned away. 'Someone's coming,' he said curtly.

Appalled, Sable pressed the back of her hand to her mouth, biting it once before she scrambled out of the hammock.

The newcomer arrived on a tractor, clearly someone from the farm. While Kain went off to talk to him Sable shot inside and splashed her face with cold water. She refused to meet her eyes in the mirror, but when she heard Kain come back she went out with head held high.

'The farm manager,' he said, examining her with a gaze clear as burnished ice. 'He's been given permission to take the quad away.'

She said abruptly, 'I want to go back to Auckland now.'

His mouth curved in a sardonic smile. 'Wiles not working, Sable?'

It took every ounce of self-control she possessed, but she parried that cynical gaze. 'I just think it's a little petty to be carrying on our private war when two boys are fighting for their lives.'

'And I think it's more than cynical of you to use their accident as an excuse.' He ignored her sudden pallor to finish, 'Very well, we'll go. Back to my apartment.'

Sable bit her lip. There was no escape; she was a prisoner of Kain's will and ruthlessness, and his flinty, formidable determination to make sure Brent didn't fall any further into her despised clutches.

Desperately she said, 'I could go to the police and tell them you're forcing me to move in with you. Or to the press.'

One black brow climbed in ironic amusement. 'And

end up in the newspapers as a hysterical idiot? I'd tell them that we quarrelled, and you were so upset you ran to them.'

They stood measuring gazes across an impassable distance. Frustration welled up inside her, and a weariness of spirit that sapped her strength. She said levelly, 'I suppose you're enjoying this.'

'No.' But his voice was uncompromising. 'If you can't take the heat, stay out of the kitchen. Obviously you saw Brent as an easy mark; he might be, but he has family who care for his welfare and won't stand by to see him stripped of his self-respect and the money he's worked so hard to earn.'

White-lipped, she said, 'I have no intention of taking him for any money.'

'Give it away,' he snarled. 'I'm not an idiot, Sable. I thought you had enough intelligence to understand that I don't do things without reason. You've already got thirty thousand dollars from Brent—'

'What?' She couldn't believe she was hearing this. 'You're mad,' she said with seething intensity. 'Quite, quite mad.'

'Are you saying he didn't buy you a diamond ring?'

Stunned, her mind whirling uselessly, she stared at him, her gaze held by the uncompromising authority of his. 'That's ridiculous,' she said numbly. 'Of course he didn't.'

Once more he employed that raised black brow to excoriating effect as he drawled, 'Try again.'

'Brent hasn't bought me anything,' she stated with passion. 'Nothing at all.'

He looked at her with sheer disgust. 'I suppose you'll be telling me next he didn't lend you money when you were kicked out of your flat?'

CHAPTER NINE

SABLE said flatly, 'No. And if he had, I'd be paying him back.'

'Not any longer.' Kain's voice was even colder. 'You're with me now, remember?'

She stared at him, then suddenly caught the implication. White-lipped, she snapped, 'You're totally disgusting. He isn't—*wasn't*—paying me to sleep with him. Brent is a gentleman.'

'In your lexicon that no doubt equates with being a sucker,' Kain said caustically. 'I am not a gentleman and I don't care what arrangement you had with Brent; if it wasn't sex for money I'll recompense him. Why were you thrown out of your flat?'

Sick at heart, she said, 'I'm surprised you don't know.'

'Tell me.'

She shrugged. 'My flatmate held a party that ended up in a minor riot—basically the flat was wrecked. My name was on the lease agreement, so I was responsible.'

'So you went weeping to Brent—'

His contemptuous tone savagely flicked a nerve. 'I did *not*.'

But in a moment of weakness she *had* told Brent about

it and then accepted his offer of shelter. Her chin came up. 'Any arrangement is between Brent and me. It's none of your business.'

'You should have realised by now that it is. You're not part of Brent's life any more. How much do you owe him?'

Seething with a bitter, hopeless defiance, she held his gaze. 'Nothing.'

His expression hardened. 'How much?'

And when she kept her lips clamped shut he said on a silky note that was more effective than any harsh sneer, 'I'll find out, Sable.'

Driven into a corner she said dully, 'I don't owe him anything. He stood guarantor for a small bank loan, which I'm paying off. To the bank, not to Brent.' She added with a spurt of anger, 'Brent is too much of a man to accept money from you, anyway.'

'But you don't really see him as a man, simply as a pigeon to be plucked. Why don't you sell the diamond ring and pay him back?'

'There is *no ring*,' she snarled, goaded beyond endurance. She stared up into his face, her eyes blazing dark fire, two spots of fire burning her cheeks. 'He *never* gave me a ring. I would *not* have accepted it from him.' She drew a ragged breath and hurled her last words at him like stones. 'You can think what you like of me, but why do you despise your cousin so much?'

His mouth hardened into a thin straight line. 'You don't know what you're talking about.'

'Are you so certain of your own infallibility that you have a completely closed mind about him too? I could— I'd like—' Horrified, she stopped before her words degenerated into incoherence.

She was standing too close to him, and, although she

was so angry she could barely articulate each intemperate word, his nearness was working some forbidden enchantment at a cellular level, weakening her so that all she could think of was a flashback to the fevered moments in his bed the previous night.

'You could do what?' he asked, a raw undernote to the words subtly defusing her anger.

How could he think of—whatever he was thinking—when she'd been so furious her brain seemed to have exploded?

His smile was dangerous, his eyes narrow and intent, and she could see the hot glitter of desire beneath his long lashes. Temptation overwhelmed anger, urging her on, demanding the easiest, most pleasurable soothing of the taut hunger that gripped her.

She should get the hell out of here before she did something else she'd despise herself for.

'Try me,' he said, that smile curling his beautiful mouth. 'Just try me, Sable.'

Quietly, each word sharp-edged as an ice crystal, she said, 'I've already tried you, remember? Last night. Once is enough.'

Too late she realised she'd flung down a direct challenge. Kain froze, every muscle in the big lean body tightening into a predatory alertness, and his eyes darkened. Danger crackled like lightning between them.

What have you done? Sable's flash of elemental anticipation turned into something perilously close to panic until she saw him reimpose control.

He stepped back and said with iron-hard dominance, 'I could make you eat those words.'

It was an uncompromising, decisive statement of fact. Sable hated him for it, but she couldn't call him a liar. One touch, one searing kiss, and incandescent passion would sweep them both into something that—for her at least—would lead to utter shame.

It took all her willpower to leash her emotions and the overdose of adrenaline pumping through her. 'This is ridiculous.' Her voice sounded creaky and she had to swallow before she could get the next words out. 'You make me so angry—but that was unforgivable.'

He shrugged and turned away. 'Get ready to leave. What do you want done with that shirt?'

'I'll wash it out before we go,' she said thinly, glad of the abrupt change of subject.

Surprisingly, most of poor Corky's blood washed away, but she knew she'd never wear the shirt again. She stowed the wet garment in the waterproof pocket in her backpack.

They drove back to Auckland in near-silence. Every nerve taut, Sable stared out through the front window, so aware of Kain she thought she could feel his aura against her skin.

Back at the apartment he showed her to a bedroom and told her unemotionally that he'd organise dinner for them in the restaurant. 'Give me the shirt,' he said.

'Why?'

He said aloofly, 'I'll get the concierge to deal with it.'

'I can—'

'Sable,' he said in a voice that sent shivers scudding the length of her spine, 'just for once, do what I suggest, all right?'

Without speaking she took out the shirt and handed it over, then waited until the door closed behind him before sitting limply down on the side of the bed.

'Dear God,' she whispered. She felt as though she'd been standing on the edge of a precipice.

She'd known Kain for such a short time, yet he'd

battered down her defences so that not only had he taken her to heaven and back in his arms, but he'd made her so angry she'd really wanted to hurt him.

A lifetime of controlling herself had rushed down the drain the moment she'd met him; she literally didn't know this woman who could spit fire and ice and vicious comments, and make love with every bit as much ferocity.

And sitting shaking on the edge of a bed wasn't going to get her ready for that sensible dinner where they'd be surrounded by people.

'Shower,' she told the alien woman inside her firmly and got to her feet.

She felt more like herself after a deluge of cold water and was bolstered further by the ritual of applying cosmetics and choosing a dress—a simple black thing, high-necked and long-sleeved. With it she wore black stockings and a pair of high-heeled black shoes.

But her heart thumped loudly when she walked along to the sitting room.

Kain was looking at some papers; he put them down when she came in and gave her a long assessing look. His expression told her that he understood why she'd worn the demure dress.

'Very appropriate,' he said, a note of cynicism hardening his tone. 'Full mourning.' And waited for a stretched moment before adding, 'With covert sexual overtones.'

Flushing, she lifted her chin a fraction of an inch. 'It has not,' she told him evenly.

'So why do I feel that I'd like to strip every last little bit of black from you—and slowly kiss every inch of the skin I reveal?' His voice was deep and sure, but beneath the sardonic words she caught that raw note that meant he was aroused.

'Because you're insatiable?' she queried with cutting, scornful emphasis.

He shrugged and glanced at his watch. 'Before we get carried away again by this war we're waging, we'd better eat.'

Obscurely disappointed, she went down with him in the private lift and into the restaurant.

Oddly—in view of the heightened emotions she'd endured in the past few hours—Sable found she was hungry. And Kain set himself to charm. Even when she disagreed with him, which she did several times, he treated her opinions with respect.

Back in the penthouse he rang his farm manager, who told him that Corky didn't seem to be too badly hurt. His brother was also improving, his condition not as serious as had first been feared.

Although the next week was frantically busy, Sable found time to visit the two patients in hospital, surprised to discover from an ebullient Corky that Kain also had visited. Not only that, he'd presented both boys with the very latest in video games. His brother had been cleared and would soon join him in the general ward.

Apart from that, she drove herself and the willing Poppy hard, dealing with the inevitable problems of changing the venue for the art auction.

'You're enjoying this, aren't you,' Poppy accused on the Friday afternoon as Sable finished a telephone call to the caterer.

'I suppose I am, even though the wretched bus company has suddenly realised they haven't got enough luxury buses for tomorrow night, but what about a double-decker to take up the slack?' Sable got to her feet and stretched luxuriously. 'Just imagine a double-decker making its way down that road! But there are always glitches.'

'And you get a kick out of fixing things.'

Surprised at the younger woman's perception, Sable said slowly, 'I suppose I do.'

Poppy grinned, then whirled when a voice from the doorway said, 'Time you went home, both of you.'

Heart pumping frantically, Sable watched her assistant's eyes widen when Kain strolled in, all sophisticated elegance in a dark, magnificently tailored business suit. She didn't blame the girl; she too was suddenly alert and excited, blood thrumming hotly through her.

God, she thought, panic-stricken, I want him so much! And he hadn't touched her once in that long week.

Kain smiled at the younger girl. 'Hello, Poppy. I believe you're doing exceedingly well here.'

Flushed, almost stammering, Poppy said eagerly, 'I'm *loving* it. Sable and I have lots of laughs, and I've never worked with someone who deals with things so efficiently before.'

'Ah, Sable is super-competent,' Kain said smoothly, his expression giving nothing away.

Sable sent him a cool glance. 'Thank you both for the vote of confidence, but at the moment I could do with less exercise of my creative talents. If one more person rings and says that they can't do what they promised I'm going to rush away and sob noisily and at great length in the cloakroom.'

Poppy gave a giggle and Kain's brows lifted. 'I'd better take you home and feed you,' he said.

Aware of Poppy's avid interest, Sable said crisply, 'I've got about half an hour's work to do here before I can leave.'

'Is the roof going to fall in if you don't do it tonight?'

Sable gave him a sharp look. What was this—a power

trip? He met her eyes with bland assurance underpinned by a steely authority.

'No, it won't,' Poppy startled her by saying in a rush. 'Dad always says that the last decision you make in the day is usually overturned the next morning. I don't even think you've had lunch, have you, Sable?'

'I can't remember,' Sable said shortly, adding, 'But your father—and Kain—' she sent him a glittering smile '—are probably right.' The smile softened when she turned it back to Poppy. 'Go on, off you go, too. You've worked hard all day, and tomorrow is going to be just frantic. I'll see you first thing in the morning at the homestead.'

Poppy fluttered her lashes at Kain. 'I'm *so* looking forward to everything,' she cooed. 'I bet it's going to be a *huge* success!'

It was. Drawn by the lure of visiting one of the most gracious houses in the country—the home of a very powerful man—more than fifty extra people had registered for the occasion, including several glamorous stars now domiciled overseas, one international racing driver, and a famous—and famously acerbic—yachtsman. The men were resplendent in evening clothes and the women had donned not only their best cocktail dresses but their most serious jewels.

The air of excitement, of eagerness, was palpable, as potent as the scent of the gardenias flowering in the garden outside. After drinking excellent cocktails and snacking on superbly prepared seafood caught that day, the guests were in the mood to play. It helped that two of them had just cashed up businesses, and as their tastes—or their art advisors' suggestions—coincided, they conducted a bidding war that sent the Foundation coffers soaring.

'The best auction we've ever had,' Mark Russell

gloated, pumping Kain's hand. 'Thanks to you, Kain. You saved our hides. It couldn't have been held in a more lovely, evocative place!'

'Or run by a more efficient events planner,' Kain said smoothly.

Mark looked astonished for a second, then recovered. 'Indeed,' he said, relinquishing Kain's hand to embrace a startled Sable and drop a kiss on her cheek. 'Well done, Sable. Not that I doubted you could pull it off—she's the best PA I've ever had,' he informed a suddenly flint-faced Kain.

'I had help,' Sable said quickly. She smiled at Poppy. 'Very good help.'

Mark looked at his flushing daughter and said in a different voice, 'Yes, I must say I've been impressed. Now, I'd better say thank you to some of these good folks. Kain, I gather your security firm has the pictures safely behind lock and key until we can get them to the new owners?'

'They're already on their way to a vault,' Kain said austerely.

Sable felt her spine stiffen as the photographer came up. She forced herself to relax. Although she didn't want to appear on the social pages again it would be good publicity, and Maire had lent her a dress that was both ultra-sophisticated and skilfully discreet.

She was on a high, elated that the whole glamorous evening had come together just as she'd imagined it. There was even a full moon, magnificent over the estuary and the islands, lending the garden its particular enchantment. Nobody wanted to go home; after Mark had announced to enthusiastic acclamation the amazing amount the auction had earned, champagne had been served, and now people were sipping and chatting, caught up in the magic of the occasion.

And through it all, Kain had been there for her, enormously sexy in the black and white of formal evening wear, his effortless charm and authority like a seal of approval for the occasion.

She cast a glance at him, her breath stopping in her throat when she caught him looking at her with a narrowed, intent gaze.

Her body came to full alert—then froze at the flash of the photographer's bulb. 'Thanks,' the man called cheerfully and disappeared into the crowd.

Awkwardly Sable said, 'Poppy, we'd better start trying to get these people onto the buses.'

An hour later the caterers finally trundled away, the housekeeper retired after a last jealous inspection of her kitchen, and Sable found herself alone with Kain. Tension gripped her, a swift sharpness that pierced every cell in her body and held her a willing captive.

He'd taken off his tie and loosened the neck of his shirt. The contrast between the white fabric and his tanned skin was so erotic she had to drag her eyes away from it.

'You look hyper,' he said, and handed her a glass of champagne. At the automatic shake of her head he said, 'It's your first for the evening, and it will help you wind down.'

She sipped the liquid, feeling the delicious stuff trickle down a throat too dry. Without looking at him she said, 'The Foundation owes you big time—if you hadn't stepped in when the Browns had to turn us down we'd have been in real trouble.'

'It was nothing,' he said coolly. '*You* pulled it off.'

'With a huge amount of help.'

He smiled. 'I don't imagine Poppy was much use.'

'Actually, that breathless little persona hides a shrewd brain, and although I have the business contacts she seems to know everyone in New Zealand who matters socially. If she didn't go to school with them then her parents or her cousins did, and between them they seem to be related to almost everyone who's anyone.'

'You sound slightly envious.'

She shrugged and put down the wine glass. 'Not really. You don't miss what you haven't had.'

'You said that once before. Do you have no relatives at all?'

'Not that I know of. My father grew up in foster homes.'

'Your mother?'

Mouth twisting, she said, 'My father never spoke of her except to say that they'd met in one of those homes, so I assume she didn't have any close relatives.'

'There are moments,' he said coolly, 'when I could— almost—find it in myself to envy you.'

Sable, who'd that very evening endured an extremely uncomfortable meeting with Brent's formidable mother, sent him a wry, amused glance. 'Moments only, I'll bet.'

What would it be like to have a family—possibly irritating, even infuriating, but always there?

Well, she wasn't ever likely to know. And this was far too intimate a conversation.

She walked across to the edge of the terrace and said, 'Thank you for everything. You'll be getting a proper letter of thanks from the Foundation, of course.'

'I don't need one.' His sounded abstracted, but when he turned her around his face was hard and honed, the eyes narrow and burnished.

Sable swallowed, and the excitement she'd managed to keep under control for the past days slipped its leash.

His hands on her shoulders tightened. 'There are other, more interesting ways of thanking someone.'

Sable knew she should fight, knew this was dangerous, but she wanted him—no, *needed* him—wrung by a hunger greater than the warnings of self-preservation.

Sighing, she yielded to that inner voice that told her this was right, that whatever happened she would never regret surrendering.

The kiss opened the floodgates of emotion; in that moment of painful revelation she knew this wasn't a facile lust, a mere animal attraction. No matter what he was, what he'd done, she loved Kain Gerard. And she would always love him.

As his mouth explored hers, she accepted her fate.

His arms hardened around her. He lifted his head and looked down at her from beneath half-closed eyelids. Lips barely moving, he said in a raw growl, 'I want you. Now.'

Wanting was safe. Wanting wasn't love. 'I want you too,' she whispered like a vow.

He picked her up and carried her into the house. In the dim haven of her bedroom he lowered her to her feet, letting her feel the fierce heat and purpose of his big, aroused body. She needed to say something—anything—but the only sound that emerged was an inarticulate murmur, soon lost against his kiss.

When he raised his head again his voice was several tones deeper. 'Much as I'd like to tear this pretty thing off you, I assume it needs to be treated with care?'

'Yes.' Desire might be clouding her brain but the dress wasn't hers. She eased herself out of the clinging silk and set it down on the blanket chest at the base of the bed.

Something wild and erotic inside her burst into flame when she heard the harsh change to his breathing. In nothing more than sleek little bra and pants, she slipped off her high-heeled sandals.

'My turn,' he said, and bent his head to kiss her shoulder.

Oh, he was so used to this; she banished the bleak little thought as one deft movement of his hands unclipped her bra. And when his teeth grazed the skin he'd kissed, little shudders of anticipation snaked down her spine.

In a smoky voice, she said, 'Take off your shirt.'

When he'd shrugged free of it she reached out to touch him, flattening her palm over the place where his heart beat heavily. His skin was hot, slightly roughened by hair—infinitely sensuous to her roaming fingertips.

Intent on what she was doing, she searched out the smooth, taut swell of muscle in one strong shoulder, then the other, following the scroll of hair that narrowed into a line pointing to the waistband of his black trousers.

'Look at me,' he commanded.

She lifted her head, and his smile thinned as he pulled her against him and took her mouth in a kiss that was both challenge and claim, a kiss that demanded everything she had to give him—and promised the same to her.

A lying kiss, because he despised her...

All conscious thought was flooded by urgent signals from Sable's body, and she sank into the turbulent seas of desire, lost to everything but the heat of Kain's passion and her own wildfire response.

Somehow she found herself on the four-poster bed watching him shuck off the rest of his clothes, her breath catching at the sight of him in the moonlight that poured through the open French doors, a sheen of silver over his shoulders and down the lean, powerful lines of his body. Her blood sang through her in a wild, siren song, and when he came down onto the bed she held out her arms to him and gave herself up to this dangerous, desperate pleasure.

Slumbrous eyes almost covered by heavy lashes, she watched the bent black head as he found her breasts with his mouth and his hands. Excitement shortened her breath, set her heart pounding in an erratic rhythm. She ran a shaking hand across his shoulders, exulting in the subtle coil and flow of the muscles beneath the sleek skin.

Already she knew this would be the last time; even if he wanted more, she'd have to reject him. Too much of his overwhelming passion, she thought with a voluptuous shudder as his lips closed around one jutting nipple, and she'd be addicted.

He lifted his head. 'Are you cold? Shall I close the doors?'

If she were any hotter she'd burst into flames. 'No,' she said drowsily, and kissed his shoulder. 'You just make me feel…so much.'

He smiled, the subtle sensation of his lips against her skin so erotic she had to catch back an involuntary groan. 'Good. Because that's how I feel too.'

He girdled her waist with a sash of kisses, then found the soft mound between her legs. Sable stiffened, but his exploration sent more excited little shudders through her. He knew what to do—how to make her feel as though she was dying of pleasure, and then, as though it wasn't enough, she needed more…

She moaned, the sudden pleading thrust of her hips taking her by surprise.

'Kain,' she whispered hoarsely, the single syllable almost broken.

'Not yet,' he told her.

Frustrated, importunate, she grabbed him and tugged him towards her.

For charged seconds they froze, staring at each other in a silent, fierce battle of wills. Then Kain said something under his breath and moved over her, thrusting into her eager body. She arched high to take him, hands linking behind his back to pull him closer, to take him inside and never ever let him go…

In perfect unison, giving and accepting at the same time, they soared through waves of ecstasy to finally reach an incandescent, rapturous climax together.

And then it was spent. Locked in his arms, Sable felt tears gather in aching intensity behind her lashes, tears of loss and longing for something that would never happen.

If only he'd stay the night with her…

But what she really wanted was for him to love her with honesty and sincerity, with everything he had and was.

As his chest stopped heaving, she thought bitterly, *Ask for him to believe your innocence, why don't you?*

It wasn't going to happen.

When he rolled over onto his back beside her she shivered, and without speaking he looped an arm around her and held her close to him. Face pressed against his shoulder, she warmed to the heat of him, the mysterious male scent that seemed to be his essence, the complete security that enveloped her.

Even as her eyes closed and the moon rode high and serene in the dark sky, she cuddled against him and sank into a voracious, draining sleep.

CHAPTER TEN

IN THE morning he was gone. Sable woke and groped for him, then gave a muffled sob and sat up. She must have slept like the dead.

She lay back onto the pillows and stared up at the elaborate plaster rose in the ceiling. Tiredly she tried to work out what to do now.

Probably the simplest way of dealing with this situation would be to tell Kain she'd fallen in love with him and wanted their affair be permanent, she thought with a bitter little smile. If she did, he'd get her out of his life so fast she'd suffer burn marks.

Or he might use her until he got tired of her and then dump her.

No, she thought wearily. He was ruthless, but she understood at some deep level that he wasn't an exploiter—not like Derek Frensham. So he wanted her, but before he embarked on satisfying that itch, he'd make sure she understood exactly what she was getting into—just like an employment contract, no doubt with a generous severance payment. Shuddering, she turned and buried her hot face into the pillow.

A loveless liaison would kill something vital in her.

After her ill-fated affair with Derek it had taken her a long time to recover her self-respect—and her feelings for Kain were so much more intense, so much more overwhelming.

Of course she could always run away. She discarded that idea swiftly. It was damned difficult to hide in New Zealand, and Kain had the power to find her quickly. Besides, the thought of retreating hurt her pride.

It was that same steely pride that got her out of bed, under the shower and into a sleek little sundress she'd found in her favourite second-hand shop.

Wincing, she looked into the mirror in the luxurious bathroom. Her mouth was fuller and more sultry than normal; her usual lipstick would emphasise those too-lush contours. After some rummaging in her make-up bag she found a gloss that offered some protection without proclaiming that she'd been well and truly loved the night before.

The house seemed silent and empty when she finally emerged, and she was greeted by the housekeeper. 'Kain's out riding,' Helen Dawson told her after one shrewd glance. 'He'll be back soon, but he said to start your breakfast without him.'

'I don't normally sleep in,' Sable said. Colour stole into her skin; was she being absurdly sensitive?

'You deserve it,' Helen said comfortably. 'You've been working really hard. It's such a gorgeous morning I set the table out on the verandah, but if you want to eat inside—'

'Oh, no—the verandah will be perfect, thank you.'

Sable went with her to the table, sheltered from the already fierce sun by a canopy of wisteria leaves. The estuary shimmered like a swathe of silk, and the sombre domes of the ancient pohutukawa trees were subtly sheened with a rusty tinge, the first indication that in a week they'd be covered in fringed flowers, cloaks of crimson and scarlet, carmine and cinnabar and vermilion—the colours of summer in this northern part of the country.

The sound of hooves turned both heads and Helen said, 'Ah, there he is—see?'

No need to ask who *he* was—the housekeeper's voice said it all. Kain rode a big chestnut with the effortless ease of someone who'd been born to the saddle.

'Can you ride?' the older woman asked conversationally.

Sable nodded. 'Not like that, however,' she said with wry honesty. 'My riding was done bareback on a neighbour's retired racehorse.'

'Kain was in the saddle before he could walk.' His housekeeper watched Kain and the horse disappear behind another clump of huge old trees. 'I'll bring you some juice.'

Sable leaned against the verandah rail, looking around. This was the more private part of the house and grounds; just through a wrought-iron fence she could see the glimmer of a swimming pool and wondered at the irony of that, with the sea only a hundred metres or so away.

She admired the huge, glossy paddles of a tree found on the offshore islands of Northland. It made a lush background to a fountain in the shape of a scallop shell. Heavy, exotic perfume from a bed of low-growing gardenias around the base of the fountain teased her nostrils; on impulse she picked one white flower and tucked it behind her ear.

Kain saw it the moment he walked out onto the verandah. She hadn't heard him, and she was standing by one of the verandah posts looking out across the estuary, so he had a good view of the white bloom glimmering in the smooth crown of her black hair.

Something about the way she leaned against the post drew his brows together. She looked too fine-drawn, almost exhausted. A fierce protectiveness weakened him; he had to stop himself from going across to slide his arms around her and lend her his strength.

Perhaps she owed that air of frailty to the scarlet-and-white sundress; it certainly showed off her slender figure to full advantage. More likely she was simply tired after weeks of hard work and frequent frustration, followed by an evening of acute tension.

Not only her work ethic impressed him. She'd showed calm competence and good humour in dealing with florists who threw nervous tantrums because they couldn't find the flowers they needed, and artists who all insisted their work be hung in the best place. She'd eased Poppy into confidence, praising her, pointing out her mistakes without humiliating her. And she'd won Helen Dawson completely over.

No wonder she was tired. When it was all over, they'd made love like tigers, her swift surrender surprising him, but not as much as her generosity and the sweet aftermath when she'd slept in his arms and he'd lain for hours, cradling her against him, reminding himself that she was a blackmailer. He'd tried to find excuses for her behaviour; she'd been young and poor, she'd had no moral upbringing...

But blackmail indicated a cold, scheming, callous mind in action.

Yet when his eyes lingered on the curve of breasts, the narrow waist and long legs, the graceful lines of her throat, all he could feel was that relentless tug of desire, an urge to forget everything he'd learned about her and take her at face value.

Some instinct must have warned her she was being

watched. She turned abruptly and saw him, and he watched colour heat those sculpted cheekbones as she stayed where she was, wary eyes scanning his face.

Kain made a decision. God knows where it would lead him. With any luck to some sort of sane resolution. But he'd heard this morning that his security men had been contacted by a victim of the blackmail attempt. Very old— and possibly too frail to be of any help, he thought grimly—Miss Popham was in a nursing home in Napier.

And now, for the first time in his life, he was torn between two courses.

'You should have slept longer,' he said and came towards her.

Sable had thought she couldn't love him any more than she already did, but she'd been wrong. He looked younger somehow in jodhpurs—still the authoritative man she loved as well as feared, but less implacable.

To her surprise, when he reached her he drew her to him and kissed her, a brief touch to her forehead that was oddly almost tender.

Stunned, she said, 'Once I wake up I can never go back to sleep so I might just as well get up.' Her voice sounded soft and husky. She hoped her skin didn't show the sensations running riot through her, summoned by that swift, almost chaste kiss.

'Did you sleep well?' He laughed softly, almost with affectionate mockery at her hot-cheeked nod. 'So did I. Come on, some breakfast will give you more energy.'

'Coffee is more likely to do the trick,' she said, stepping away from him because she couldn't think, couldn't do anything but remember, and those memories were too intrusive, too potent—and so hopeless she didn't want to face them.

'Do you want me to change?' he asked. 'I imagine I still smell of horse.'

Smiling, she let her eyes roam his powerful body. 'Not much. Besides, I like it and you look great in jodhpurs.'

After breakfast he took her sailing to a lonely island off the coast where the wind played with the cottontail grass and the waves lapped against a beach that was pink as a quiet dawn.

They swam ashore and there, beneath the welcoming arms of a pohutukawa, they made love again. Sable knew she was riding into danger, but if this was all there was to be for her then she would take it eagerly. Her life for the past eight years seemed empty and cold in comparison; it would be so again, but she'd always have this—memories of passion from a man who couldn't love her.

Memories wouldn't keep her warm at night, or tease her or make her laugh, or intrigue her into hotly arguing as she'd done with Kain more times than was sensible, but memories were more than she'd ever expected to have.

That night they drove back to Auckland. He waited until she'd unpacked before opening a bottle of champagne.

Only the best, she thought ironically with a glance at the label. 'What is this for—the successful auction? We drank to that last night.'

'No,' he said calmly. 'This is to a new start.'

An irrational hope tore at Sable. Harshly she said, 'I don't know what you mean.'

'It's quite simple,' Kain told her, his eyes cool as they scanned her face. 'You want me. I want you. Together we're amazingly compatible. It makes sense for you to stay with me.'

Her heart broke, shattered by the calm pragmatism of

his words. If she did what she wanted to—throw a scream-ing, raging tantrum to hide her bitter desolation—he'd realise how hurt she was by his callous assumption that she could be bought so easily.

'Just like that?' she asked in a brittle voice. 'The sex is good so we stay together? And when we get bored with each other we say goodbye and go our separate ways, no bones broken?'

His brows rose. 'Of course, I would look after you,' he said, a note of steel beneath the courteous tone.

Pride overrode everything else. This time she'd try for some dignity. 'No,' she said quietly. 'I'm not good mistress material.'

He smiled. 'You're far too modest,' he drawled. 'You're superb mistress material—wanton, sexy as hell, a generous lover. You look superb on my arm. You're in-telligent, have excellent manners, and you throw bril-liant parties. And you're never boring. What more could any man want?'

His taunts stung, but they stiffened her resolve. 'I don't know what men want, unless it's just a warm body in a bed. But I haven't heard anything in your comprehensive list that *I* might want.' She cast a scathing glance at the bottle of champagne. 'So you'll have to drink that by yourself.'

'I don't drink alone.' He sounded reflective, and she wondered what was going on behind that arrogantly handsome face. 'As for what men want—I've already detailed it, but perhaps I missed something. As well as all the rest, I want a lover who turns to fire in my arms. And you do that too.'

'No!' This time there was a note of panic in her voice, but when she looked up he hadn't moved. She tried to feel relieved—she *was* relieved—but she hadn't realised until that moment how much she'd wanted to be wooed into surrender.

Even if it was only sexual surrender, without love, without commitment.

He was honest, she thought achingly, tempted unbearably to take what he offered, to know for a few short months the joy of being Kain's lover.

No, not his *lover*—his mistress, bought and paid for, an ornament in public, a trophy in his bed, and eventually nothing in his life.

'No,' she said again, more steadily this time. 'And before you say anything more, yes, I know you could force me to—'

'I don't rape.' He ground the words out between his teeth.

White-faced, she said, 'It wouldn't be rape and you know it. But for me it's nothing more than an inconvenient lust, something to be sated quickly and without emotion, something I resent so much it would eventually become a wasteland for me.'

His eyes narrowed. 'Why, Sable?'

Vehemently she said, 'I've already been there—'

And stopped, catching back the tumbling words. But she'd said too much; she could sense his keen interest and wondered what was going on in that coldly incisive brain.

More temperately she said, 'Don't you think there should be some sort of respect between lovers? Sex without emotion is just a mechanical urge to satisfy an itch. I want more than that.' She lifted her head and looked at him with pride. 'I *deserve* more than that.' And before she had time to think again she added, 'And so do you.'

For long seconds he looked at her, blazing eyes screened by his lashes, his face impassive, yet she sensed the immense force of his will leashing emotions she couldn't discern. The silence lasted too long, became charged with tension that sawed at her nerves and blocked the breath in her throat. What was he thinking behind that handsome mask?

Eventually he said calmly, 'Very well, then.' He shrugged. 'But you stay here until I'm sure Brent no longer hankers after you.'

Sable's glance at his unsparing face told her this wasn't negotiable. Heart twisting painfully, she nodded. 'All right.'

To her astonishment he held out his hand. 'So it's a bargain.'

Her skin tingled when they shook hands, but she felt oddly light-headed, as though she'd finally managed to dent the coldly dispassionate attitude that saw her as a pawn to be used and manipulated rather than a woman with feelings and pride.

Though his dislike and distrust were clearly still intact. After all, she thought with bitter irony, who could trust a blackmailer?

The following few days were still tense, but she thought they forged a fragile peace between them. They went out twice, the first time to a formal dinner with a Singaporean business delegation. Sable hoped she acquitted herself well enough to pass muster.

Certainly no one would know from the guests' perfect manners if she hadn't.

Kain said nothing. It hurt and humiliated her that she wanted him to acknowledge…

What? That she fitted into his world?

'But you don't. You don't have the jewellery for it, to start with,' she told her reflection as she creamed off her make-up. The tycoon from Singapore had been accompanied by his daughter, whose diamonds had outshone the chandeliers.

The second function was a cocktail party held at a vast, overornate mansion on the cliffs above one of Auckland's most popular beaches. Sable knew Kain was bored even though his demeanour showed no sign of it. She was bored too; the people seemed dull, the evening lagged, and she had the misfortune to meet someone from her past.

It was particularly painful that it should be this woman, who could barely hide her surprise at seeing Sable there— or her desire to meet Kain.

When Sable introduced them, Kain was charming and aloof, but once the conversation was over and the woman had gone back to her group he looked at Sable. 'Old enemy?'

He saw too much. 'Not exactly,' she said scrupulously. 'I didn't move in her circles, but her daughter was in my class in primary school. She once insisted—in front of everyone in the class—that her daughter had caught nits from me. I'm sure she was hugely relieved when the girl went off to boarding school the next year.'

His mouth compressed. 'I can understand kids being cruel,' he said curtly, 'but that was vicious.'

She shrugged. 'It happens when your father is the town drunk.' She flashed a wry smile. 'And I have to admit it gave me a certain nasty satisfaction tonight to see her so flustered when she realised I was with you.'

'Glad to be of use.' His grin somehow eased the smart of the old shame, and when he took her hand and held it she felt the last lingering vestiges disappear. 'But it's more likely that she was impressed at your sophistication and didn't have the wit or the manners to hide it.'

God, but she loved him...

In spite of everything.

Later, emerging from the cloakroom, she saw the woman talking earnestly to Kain. She was flushed, and there was something about the way she looked around that made Sable stiffen. Or perhaps it was Kain's face—coldly remote and arrogant.

As she threaded her way across the crowded room she wondered bleakly if she'd ever be able to put the past behind her.

By the time she reached Kain he was alone again, and he didn't mention the conversation. Neither did Sable, although anger burned in her like a dark fire. After all, the woman couldn't have added anything more than gossip to Kain's information.

A few minutes later she was temporarily alone when she noticed the woman making her way towards her. As she came up the woman glanced around the room, then half hissed beneath her breath, 'I actually used to feel sorry for you, you know. Not now, though—you two deserve each other.'

She brushed past before Sable could ask her what she meant, but she deduced that Kain had slapped her attempt at mischief-making down, and felt a forbidden warmth in her heart.

The next day they went up to the bach and she was surprised to realise that although they were scrupulously careful not to touch each other and tension was ever-present, he seemed to be intent on establishing some kind of connection between them beyond the merely physical. They talked a lot, and he showed her how to surf. He was a patient teacher, and when at last she stood up and rode her first small wave onto the beach, he congratulated her with as much pleasure as if she'd caught a big one.

He'd be a good father, she thought as they drove back to the penthouse. An odd, highly suspicious mixture of regret and desire warred for supremacy as she warned herself not to even *think* things like that.

That week a cyclone in the Pacific, the first of the summer, led to the hurried deployment of nurses and doctors and stores. Efficiently Sable geared up for the extra work, only relaxing late on the Friday when her part in the exercise was over and she was alone, able to get on with more mundane work.

Almost immediately, the telephone on her desk rang again.

'What *now*?' she demanded silently of the universe before answering, 'Sable Martin.'

There was silence at the other end, and then a voice she'd hoped never to hear again said, 'Hi, Sable. Long time no see.'

'Derek?' she asked incredulously, an icy pool opening up beneath her ribs.

'Derek Frensham. The very same.' He laughed. 'Interesting to see your photo splashed through the Sunday papers again this week with the billionaire you're shacked up with. No—' divining what she intended to do '— don't hang up on me, sweets. Not a wise move.'

'What's this all about?' she asked brusquely.

'Let's just say I'm catching up. You're obviously doing really, really well, but things aren't too good for me.'

Feeling sick, she forced herself to say, 'I'm not at all sorry. You damned near got me put in prison.'

'Oh, come on, now, that was just a mistake on my grandfather's part. But that's all in the past now. How about we meet and talk over old times?'

'No,' she said shortly.

'I think you should.'

The threat hung in the air. Well, blackmail was his thing; he probably wanted money, she thought, and the nausea grew into something perilously close to panic.

He was clear out of luck; she had nothing. She said coldly, 'Why should I? The last time I listened to you I lost my job and my reputation.'

'But I saved your hide,' he said indignantly. 'I took the rap for you because I knew my grandfather would call the cops if he knew it was you.' His voice got louder and more righteous. 'I did all that for you, and then you bloody left me, and the old man disowned me. You owe me for that, Sable.'

Had he always spoken like a gangster from a B movie? Despising herself for once thinking he was wonderful, she said through gritted teeth, 'He didn't call the police because he *knew* that you used me to get to his files so you could blackmail those poor people—one of whom committed suicide, remember.'

'Oh, I remember, but not the way you do—and who's going to believe the daughter of a local alcoholic?' he sneered.

Who indeed?

He broke into her frantically racing thoughts with a curt, 'I need money. Now.'

'Even if I had any, I wouldn't give it to you—'

'Then I'll have to think about letting your tame billionaire know all about you. Wonder which one of us he'd believe?'

Sable flinched, but what did his threat matter? She couldn't sink any lower in Kain's estimation. She opened her mouth to call Derek's bluff, only to be struck dumb by a futile combination of outrage and frustration and sick humiliation.

'And I'll bet that bunch of do-gooders you work for would be interested to know about your past.' He paused. 'You'd probably be able to lay your hands on some of the spare cash they've got lying around. That auction you organised collected more than three million dollars—'

'You are *despicable*,' she said harshly.

He whined, 'I'm desperate. And if you can't get it from them, you'd better earn some more on your back from your tame billionaire while you can. I need money and I need it now.'

She crashed the receiver down. When the telephone rang again she flinched, staring at it as though it was a snake. It rang again; she picked it up, heard him say, 'Don't you—' and hung up immediately, checking his number. He kept on ringing. She ignored each call.

By the time she was free to leave she was exhausted and oddly afraid. Worriedly she gathered her things and went out and down into the foyer.

Where the first person she saw was Kain, talking to a blushing Poppy.

The pang of jealousy that tore through her shocked her. She had to stop and take a deep, slow breath, unclench her jaw, and paste on a serene expression that made her face ache.

Kain saw her coming above Poppy's head—calm, composed, her walk as graceful as ever—and had to repress a violent rush of hunger. This past week had been sheer hell; every second, every minute he'd needed her, cursing himself for being stupid enough to state his terms so bluntly that pride had driven her to fling his offer in his face.

He looked down at Poppy's pretty, animated face as she gushed, 'And she's so patient and kind; when she's supervising me she doesn't treat me like a total idiot and she makes me feel as though I can do *anything*. Some of the staff think I'm just a daddy's girl wasting their time. I'm going to university next year—Sable said it's a good thing to do because it shows you can work hard and organise your life.'

'It does,' he said, his gaze drifting back to Sable walking towards them.

Poppy turned and grinned. 'Hi, Sable, I'm just telling your man how wonderful you are.'

A faint colour stained Sable's high cheekbones. 'I hope not,' she said lightly.

Poppy laughed. 'If you don't want hero-worship you shouldn't be so darned nice,' she said cheerfully. 'Oh, there's Dad. Better go—I want to talk him into something, and it's going to take the whole trip home to do it.'

She rushed off, leaving Kain looking down at the calm face that belied Sable's inner tension. Once they were in the car he said, 'What's the matter?'

'Nothing,' she said automatically. 'I'm just wondering why you came to pick me up.'

Without expression he said, 'Brent's home.'

Her stomach hollowed out. 'But I thought he was going to be away for much longer.'

'He got off the barquentine in the Caribbean and flew back.'

'Why?'

His glance was laced with irony. 'Guess, Sable.'

She bit her lip. 'Have you seen him?'

'Not yet.' He sounded aloof, a bit fed up.

Bully for him, she thought savagely.

Her heart contracted. She didn't want to hurt Brent, but if he thought he loved her it would be kinder in the long run. Against the golden haze of a summer afternoon Kain's profile was slashing and forceful, entirely lacking in gentleness.

But he could be gentle... The vagrant thought popped into her brain, and with it the memory of their lovemaking. He had never used his great strength against her.

That ever-present ache deep in her loins heated into active longing. Dismissing it, she concentrated on the forthcoming uncomfortable interview with Brent. She owed him that.

'So what's happening?' she asked thinly.

'He's coming around later.'

'I want to see him alone.'

'No,' he said.

Sable's hackles lifted. Keeping her voice steady with an effort she said, 'I know you don't care about humiliating me, but Brent is your cousin. He deserves better from you than that.'

His mouth hardened. 'No. He needs to know there is no hope for him and he can only do that by seeing us together.'

'But—'

His tone was inflexible. 'I'm not prepared to negotiate on this.'

'Are you ever prepared to negotiate?' she asked bitterly.

He paused, and she looked up, startled to see his jaw harden. 'You have every right to ask that,' he said abruptly, 'but now isn't the time to discuss it. Do I have your agreement to see Brent with me in the room?'

'Yes,' she said in bitter surrender. 'If you don't care what your cousin thinks of you, why should I?'

Brent arrived ten minutes after they got back to the apartment. Sable had changed into a pair of cotton trousers and a shirt, slipped her feet into light sandals and then renewed her make-up, examining her face carefully in the bathroom mirror to make sure the mask was flawless.

Amazing, she thought grimly, turning away to look at the luxury around her.

Memories of the house she'd shared with her father— a tumbledown place that had been slowly disintegrating

around them, made her choke back a half-sob. Taking a
deep breath, she walked out into the hall and along to the
sitting room.

CHAPTER ELEVEN

WITH nerves screwed up to such a pitch she almost felt ill, Sable walked through the door. Both men swung around at her entrance. Side by side, the family resemblance was almost startling. Kain was taller, but somehow Brent seemed to have grown—matured and broadened—in the few weeks he'd been away.

As she came in Kain turned his head and said, 'Here she is.'

For a wistful, painful second she found herself wishing he'd always use that voice—warm, appreciative, almost tender—when he spoke to her.

He moved to her and took her arm, not holding her too close or too obviously, but subtly exhibiting all the signs of a dominant male with the woman he'd claimed for his own.

Sable smiled at Brent. 'Hello.'

After a moment's keen scrutiny of them both, he said neutrally, 'Hi, how are you?'

'Fine, thank you. And you?'

Stiff, too formal, but she couldn't relax.

Eyes watchful, Brent said, 'Having a ball.' He switched his gaze to his cousin. 'So why did you bring me here?'

Ignoring Sable's muffled gasp, Kain said crisply, 'To prove a point.'

Brent shrugged. 'Done it?'

Looking at Sable, Kain said calmly, 'You tell me.'

His cousin frowned. 'You treat her well, OK, or answer to me. Sable's special.'

He'd managed to startle Kain; she felt the swift tension in his muscles. *Good*, Sable thought, hugely relieved. It served Kain right to be tipped off his arrogant pedestal.

But what on earth had persuaded him to do this?

Brent said, 'Knowing you, Kain, I'll bet you had her investigated.' Unaware of Sable's sudden rigidity, he went on, 'I'm glad you didn't let that business years ago put you off, but you'd know it was all lies anyway.'

'Yes,' Kain said crisply, a note in his voice making Sable stare at him. He met her gaze with a cool warning. 'How did you find out about it?'

'Sorry, Sable, but I had you investigated.' Brent sent an apologetic glance at Sable's shocked face before transferring it to his cousin. In a voice that verged on aggressive he went on, 'It came up, of course. But I knew something about the Frenshams. You remember Blossom McFarlane—Mum's friend? One of the twinset and real pearls brigade from Hawkes Bay? Well, I went to school with her son, and his older brother had been in the same class as Derek Frensham. He knew what sort of person Derek was—used to regale us with tales of his schemes. He came across as a total cad, so when I found out that he'd been around while Sable was supposed to have blackmailed two of the local residents I guessed that somehow he was tied up in it. When I found out old Mr Frensham had tidied up the situation, I was sure of it.'

'I see.'

Brent shrugged and looked back at Sable. 'Sorry I pried. It made me feel a bit queasy, but—well, in my business I had to have trustworthy people around me and I guess the suspicion somehow leaked over into my private life...' Clearly uncomfortable, he asked, 'How did you two guys meet?'

'At the races,' Kain said dryly, his tone giving nothing away. 'She was modelling one of Maire's outfits—and she should have won, but they went for Jen Purviss-Jones instead.'

The two men exchanged looks. 'All bubble and bounce, the epitome of youthful exuberance,' Brent agreed, the irony in his tone making him sound for a second like his cousin. He grinned at them both and asked hopefully, 'Are we going out to dinner?'

Kain saved Sable from having to answer. 'You're leaving again tomorrow, aren't you?'

'Yep.'

'Then you'd better have dinner with your mother,' Kain said.

He said gloomily, 'I suppose. She's going to give me the full X-ray, though.'

Something about Brent's demeanour and his tone caught Sable's attention. He'd met a girl, she realised, her jumble of relief and surprise and shock tempered by amusement. Keeping her gaze away from Kain she said demurely, 'Of course she will. She'll want to spend as much time with you as she can. But before you go, tell us all about her.'

Colouring, Brent ran a hand through his hair and gave a half-smile. 'Mum?'

Sable laughed. 'Come on, own up. Who is she and would I like her?'

'Yeah, you would,' he said eagerly. 'How did you know

I'd met someone? She's gorgeous—she comes from South Africa and she grew up on a game farm. When I finish the trip on the boat I think I'll head across there. I'd really like to go on safari and Laura says her family do exceptionally good ones.'

'It sounds fantastic,' Sable said, still not looking at Kain.

What would he do now? Kick her out?

A pang of such pain shot through her that it was all she could do to stand up straight. As though Kain had felt it, the fingers on her arm tightened in support.

She said quietly, 'Brent, do you think you might tell Kain who you bought the diamond ring for?'

Brent stared at her, then demanded, 'How did you know about—?'

'Your mother told me,' Kain said, his voice deep and confident. He added, 'You gave her address to the jeweller and the valuation documents went to her. She didn't even look at the address until after she'd read the valuation.'

Brent swore beneath his breath, then looked shame-faced. 'Sorry, Sable. I meant it to be a surprise,' he said. 'Damn, I went to such lengths—I had to filch a wedding photo of Mum and Dad, and blow it up so the jeweller could see what her engagement ring looked like. You remember, Kain, she lost it just after Dad died, and I told her then that when I had the money I'd buy her a new one. Well, I had the money, and I got one made. I was going to give it to her on the anniversary of their wedding when I came back. I never thought of the valuation papers going to her. Blast!'

Sable said warmly, 'Go straight home and give it to her now. She'll cry all over you but hey, you can cope with that.'

Half an hour later—time spent mainly in listening to

Brent's praise of his new love and the trip on the barquentine—he left, promising to send them postcards from every port.

Sable had grown increasingly strained; although Brent hadn't seemed to notice, Kain had been strangely quiet. Perhaps he was wondering how to get her out of his life now that Brent no longer fancied himself in love with her—if he ever had.

Well, Kain didn't have to worry. She'd leave tonight, before he realised the true nature of her feelings for him.

When the door finally closed behind the two men she went into her room and fought back stupid tears as she began throwing clothes into her backpack.

She'd almost finished when from the doorway Kain said in tones of ice, 'What the hell do you think you're doing?'

'Leaving.' Expression under such control the muscles in her face ached, she looked up. 'You can't keep me here any longer,' she said, salvaging pride by pre-empting his marching orders.

His eyes narrowed. 'Oh, yes, I can,' he said silkily.

Shocked, she stared at him. 'But Brent's obviously no longer in any danger from me—not that he ever was. I hope you're satisfied of that now. He even knew about the blackmail.'

Just *saying* it made her feel dirty. She added on a snap, 'And the diamond ring is no longer an issue.'

'This new relationship could well be a face-saving exercise. You'll stay here as my lover until I'm convinced Brent no longer harbours any hopes.' He looked at her backpack. 'So you can put that away.'

Sable seethed, anger contesting for advantage over a deeply shameful relief. Grimly, her voice shaking, she said, 'I will never forgive you for this.'

She turned and stalked across to the door, furious all over again when she heard him say with amusement, 'Brent really doesn't know how lucky he is. I've saved him from a termagant.'

'I'm only like this with—' She stopped precipitately. Admitting that he was the only person who'd ever made her this angry was revealing too much. 'With people I despise,' she finished triumphantly and hurled the door shut behind her.

Only when she found herself in the hall outside did she realise that she'd left him in her bedroom.

OK, so she'd made a total fool of herself. *Face it*, she said to the part of her that was quivering with embarrassment. She opened the door again.

Kain hadn't moved and was looking down at her backpack with a grim expression. It vanished when she came back into the room, his brow climbing with familiar irony.

She said quietly, 'Please go now.'

He strolled towards her, something in his gait setting off alarm sirens. Resisting the urge to put up her arms against him, she stared at him with all the defiance she could muster.

'When you're angry your eyes glitter with dark fire,' he said conversationally. He bent his head and closed them with a soft kiss each. 'And your mouth is ripe and red and eminently kissable, even when it's spitting fire.'

Body tense and reckless, she waited for him to kiss her properly. When nothing happened, shame forced her lashes upwards to meet a humourless smile.

'But you're tired, and I'll bet you didn't have any lunch. Unpack while I order dinner. We'll eat in and you can go to bed early. And if I can't trust you to eat regular meals in future I'll tell young Poppy to see that you do.'

He would too, and Poppy was so dazzled she'd nag

until Sable ate. Sombrely, an aching emptiness where her heart should be, she watched him leave the room.

What kind of hypnotic spell had Kain enmeshed her in? Even when she was furious with him she still wanted him.

There could be no future for them. OK, so the mystery of the diamond ring had been solved, but that blackmail charge stood between them like a barred gate.

Unless Brent's artless testimony had changed Kain's opinion of her? It just might, she thought longingly.

And it might not too. Sable had only realised she was free of suspicion during a painful interview with Mr Frensham when he'd—*almost*—admitted that his grandson had been caught actually contacting another person to blackmail.

Anyway, more than anything, she wanted Kain to believe in her innocence without demanding proof.

Oh, why not cry for the moon? She had a better chance of getting that than expecting Kain to trust her...

She sat down on the bed, eyes travelling to the backpack stuffed with her clothes. It was time she faced facts. This hungry obsession couldn't be love—surely that was much more gentle, a kinder emotion than the reckless passion that consumed her?

She wasn't even sure she *liked* Kain. Not as she liked Brent anyway, who was, she thought with a sad little smile, going to make some extraordinarily fortunate woman a wonderful husband one day.

Apart from all that bitter baggage, she and Kain had absolutely nothing in common. Yet whenever she thought of him her heart sang a wild, primeval song. Just looking at him sent her pulse rate soaring, and although he made her so angry she could barely control herself, he also made her feel more acutely alive than ever before.

And she had to admire his iron-bound sense of honour,

his flinty determination to protect his more vulnerable cousin—so many things about him.

Grim-faced, Sable sorted her clothes back into drawers and the wardrobe. Actually, they did have something in common—fantastic sex. But she was mature enough to know that even though he managed through some unkind quirk of fate and genes to rouse a part of her that had never existed before, a real relationship needed much more than mind-blowing passion.

Firmly repressing memories of interesting conversations with him, she reapplied her lipstick and went out, determined to ignore the simmering heat of repressed passion.

He'd been speaking on the telephone, but he hung up as she came into the room.

Sable looked at him, eyes lingering on the angular alignment of his strong features, the tall, lithe figure and the potent male charisma, and in an instant endured a kind of rearrangement of herself, a massive shift in consciousness.

In that moment, as he looked gravely at her, she knew that all her protestations, her self-serving evasions, meant nothing. She loved him; she would love him until she died.

It was wonderful and it hurt so much she could barely breathe with the glory and the pain—the utter hopelessness—of it.

He said, 'I owe you an apology. Several, actually, but this is the first one.'

Her brows climbed. She caught her breath and said unevenly, 'I must admit life with you is never dull—there's something new every day.'

His smile was part amusement, part cynicism. 'Enjoy it—I have as little taste as anyone for admitting I'm wrong, but I was wrong when I accused you of accepting the ring from Brent.'

Sweet relief flooded her, but she held it back; the diamond ring had only been a side issue. And one glance at his uncompromising face told her that nothing had really changed. Shrugging, she said, 'It's not really important, is it?'

His lashes drooped. 'I dislike making mistakes.'

'Is that why you're sorry? If you *are* sorry?'

'I am sorry,' he said briefly. 'Extremely sorry. I should have checked further before accusing you.'

What she really wanted to hear was that he didn't believe her capable of accepting a diamond ring worth thirty thousand dollars from a man she didn't intend to marry. But that wasn't going to happen.

A humourless smile twisted her mouth. 'Apology accepted with about as much reluctance as you made it.'

'Ungraciously given, ungraciously accepted?'

They measured each other like opponents and then he held out his hand. In quite a different voice, he said, 'You told me I was the only man to make you so angry—you're the only woman I've ever jumped to so many conclusions about. And for that I'm sorry too.'

She bit her lip and said quietly, 'I suppose I should say it's all right, but—it hurt.'

'I heartily and unconditionally apologise for doing that.' Before she could say anything he continued, 'Did you get a phone call from Derek Frensham today?'

Shock robbed her of an answer at first, and when she did speak her voice sounded strangely disconnected, almost detached. 'Did he ring you too?'

'Just before I left the office.'

'Oh, God, I'm so sorry you were bothered by him,' she

said unevenly, nausea chilling her. 'I suppose he wanted money.'

He shrugged, but that penetrating gaze never left her. 'He did.'

Sable closed her eyes in mortification. 'What did he say?'

Almost casually Kain said, 'He threatened to expose you as a blackmailer and a liar, and me as an idiot who'd been stupid enough to get tangled up with the wrong woman.'

'Up to his old tricks. I hope you told him to go to hell,' she said, her voice brittle and strained.

'Of course.' He paused, his relentless gaze on her face, then said evenly, 'Before we go any further with this, tell me exactly what happened when you left school to work for Frensham's grandfather.'

She bit her lip, afraid to look at him. Only the truth would satisfy him—and she needed to tell him, although she already knew he wouldn't believe her. 'Why should I? You told me you didn't need to listen to my lies, and it doesn't seem as though you've changed your mind. I'd prefer not to discuss it.'

'I don't blame you for that,' he said, 'but this time there will be no accusations.'

She met his gaze warily, and he went on, 'You accused me of not listening to you, and you were right. I'm ready to listen now.'

Sable took a deep breath, gathering courage around her like a cloak. This might be her only chance. 'After my father died I was…lost. I'd always looked after him, you see. Mr Frensham dealt with Dad's estate—the insurance money. I wanted to use some of it to pay off Dad's debts, but he'd left it to me on the condition I used it for further education, and Mr Frensham was the executor and wouldn't release it. The woman who worked for him had just taken maternity leave. I had good computer skills, so he offered me the temporary job. It—came at the right time. I wanted to get a tertiary qualification, and I knew if I saved everything I could just manage to pay off Dad's debts before the beginning of the academic year.'

She paused, gathering her courage.

'Go on,' Kain said calmly.

'Then Derek came to stay with his grandfather.' The heat of embarrassment faded into pallor, but she went on steadily, 'He made a play for me and I was dazzled. We became lovers.'

'How old was he?'

Astonished, she looked at him, recognised the cold distaste in his eyes, and winced. 'Late twenties, I think. Perhaps coming up thirty. Why?'

'He was a swine,' he said with an aloof lack of expression.

'Yes, well, as I said, I was flattered.' Shamed, she dragged in a deep breath. 'And I desperately needed someone to love right then. He took to coming into the office quite frequently and while he waited for his grandfather to finish with a client he used to rummage around in the files. I told him he shouldn't, but he just laughed it off and I—I didn't realise what he was doing.'

She paused, then said abruptly, 'I was so stupidly besotted I didn't even tell Mr Frensham. Then…then I was accused of using information from the files to blackmail two of his clients.' She stopped, took a breath, and controlled her shaking voice. 'I knew I hadn't done it, so it could only have been Derek. I was shattered, especially when Mr Frensham didn't believe me. And of course gossip raced around the district; I think Derek started it, but it was—horrible, especially after the first man Derek approached committed suicide. And I felt guilty too—for not telling Mr Frensham about Derek poking around.'

She stopped, realising that she was wringing her hands. Clenching them, she went on tonelessly, 'But in the end something happened—I don't know what—and Mr Frensham told me he no longer believed I had anything to do with it.'

'What convinced the solicitor that it **was his** grandson?' Stone-faced, his voice equally inexpressive, he was watching her closely.

'I don't know, but I think—I heard—that Derek had been in trouble before.'

'What happened afterwards?' Kain's tone was coolly implacable.

'Mr Frensham had a heart attack and died. Derek disappeared. I left and went to Auckland and found myself a job packing shelves in the supermarket. I've never been back.' She finally looked defiantly at him.

Still she could learn nothing from his handsome, unreadable face. His mouth was hard, his whole attitude inflexible.

Wearily she said, 'I wish you hadn't got tangled up in the whole nasty business.'

His expression altered a fraction. 'Do you know where Frensham is?'

On a shudder she said, 'No. In Auckland, I assume. Why?'

'It's just as well,' he said remotely. 'If I knew where he was I'd be tempted to track him down and kill him.'

Not daring to believe she'd heard what he said, she stared at him. 'I don't understand.'

'It's quite simple,' he said, still in that flat, lethal tone. 'I would very much like to tear him into small pieces for what he did to you—and what he's trying to do now. And because I believed the gossip and the scandal too easily— but that's my guilt, not his.'

Her eyes enormous in her face, Sable felt a faint glow of hope build in her breast.

Kain's smile was twisted, his expression wry. 'At least as soon as I realised that you were not a viciously amoral creature intent on stripping Brent of his hard-earned capital gains, I did dig deeper—and got nowhere.'

Despair gripped her hard. 'I don't suppose it matters.'

'Does the name Miss Popham mean anything to you?'

Her eyes, wide and shocked, flew to his flat grey gaze. 'I—yes, of course. She used to live next door—she was good to me.'

And the wild gossip mill in that small district had fingered the elderly woman as Derek's second blackmail victim, tongues running riot with whispered surmises about her past.

'Apparently she heard about my investigator's questions and has been trying to contact me.' He was watching her with cool speculation.

Numbly she said, 'I thought she was dead.'

He gave a short, humourless crack of laughter. 'Far from it. She's in a retirement home in Napier.'

Sable felt her head whirl. 'And what—what did she say?'

'Nothing—I haven't spoken to her.'

Sable looked vaguely around, saw a chair, and collapsed into it. A kind of feverish hope tangled her emotions so violently that she could barely ask, 'Why not?'

He poured her a glass of water and said, 'Here, drink this.'

And when half of it had gone down he said, 'I don't know exactly when I realised that I had the wrong idea about you.' Without altering the tone, he went on, 'I do know that if I hadn't taken one look at you and wanted you so much I could hardly control myself, I'd probably have been much more reasonable about everything.'

He paused, then went on deliberately, 'My father and mother fought like cat and dog. They adored each other—never looked at anyone else—but they didn't seem to be able to live happily and serenely together. I grew up in constant turmoil. As soon as I was old enough to think about marriage, I decided I wasn't going to live like that.'

Sable had to take in a jagged breath before she could say in a remote little voice, 'Yes, I understand.'

His smile was twisted by rueful self-derision. 'I deliberately chose lovers who were serene and composed, who made no demands on me. And then you exploded into my life, and I wanted you as much as I despised you, so I used your supposed past sins as a defence against admitting the truth.'

'The—truth?' she croaked, heart pounding so heavily in her ears that she had to watch his beloved mouth to make out the words.

And even then she didn't—couldn't—believe them.

'I love you,' he said without inflexion. His eyes narrowed. 'No sensible person believes in love at first sight, but that's what happened.' He waited and when she still stared at him without answering, he drawled, 'This is where you tell me that you wouldn't have me if I was the last man in the world.'

Unsteadily she blurted, 'Can we just take it as read?' And burst into tears.

His arms closed around her, warm, strong, infinitely protective, and she choked out against his chest, 'I don't know—I'm so happy, but now I c-c—I can't—'

'Hush,' he said, his voice deep and oddly shaken. 'Just tell me whether or not you love me.'

'Of course I do!'

He let out a long breath. Astounded, she looked up and met his eyes, saw there a flash of vulnerability that wrenched her heart. 'I hoped you did,' he said, fishing out a handkerchief. 'Here, you're soaking me.' And when she just cried harder he said gently, 'Sable, I love you with everything I have, everything I am, but I'm not ever going to be able to tell you again if this is your reaction. Hearing you cry shreds my heart.'

'I c-can't s-stop,' she wailed, grabbing the handkerchief and trying to mop up. 'I never c-cry. I d-don't know how to prove that, but I do love you so m-much.'

'I don't need proof,' he said and removed the cloth from her hands, tenderly wiping the tears away. 'That's what I'm trying to tell you—I believe unreservedly and without any limits that you had absolutely nothing to do with that old blackmail case—that it simply isn't in you to think like that.'

He picked her up and carried her across to the sofa, lowering himself into it so he could arrange her comfortably in his arms.

For long moments they sat locked together, and Sable let herself believe, cautiously at first, but the solid thudding of his heart, his closeness and tenderness finally calmed her enough for her to be able to ask huskily, 'So why did you bring Brent back?'

He didn't immediately answer, and once again she lifted her eyes and caught that fleeting, startling flash of nakedness, a glimpse into a man whose natural dominance could be threatened by love.

His mouth twisted. 'I was—jealous, I suppose.' The muscles in his broad shoulders flexed as he went on, 'Yes, jealous. It's a novel emotion for me, not one I recognised straight away, and when I did I resented it, but I needed to see you together, to know that you felt nothing more for him than the friendship you claimed.'

'And now?'

He tilted her chin and looked at her, his gaze intent and searching, his voice very deep and sure. 'I'm convinced. I suppose I just needed the *i*'s dotted where my cousin was concerned.'

'So why the fuss about me leaving just now?'

His eyes darkened. 'I couldn't bear to lose you—I just reacted instead of thinking.'

She said quietly, 'It was tearing me apart.' But she needed to know more, to understand how a man who seemed to believe the worst of her could reluctantly learn to trust her and his own deepest instincts. 'Kain, what made you believe me? You were so convinced I was the worst sort of cheat—what made you change your mind?'

He closed his eyes for a second, then opened them, hard as diamonds, the piercing gaze shot with a glimmer of wry humour. 'Actually, I started to believe you couldn't have done it when we first made love.'

Eyes widening to their fullest extent she took this in, then sat bolt upright. 'You could tell I wasn't a blackmailer because I was good in bed?' she demanded, unable to work out whether she was delighted or furious.

He laughed and kissed her into silence. 'You were utterly, wholly generous, you gave me everything without reservation. And when you climaxed in my arms you were totally shocked. I realised you'd never had an orgasm before, and that you were completely inexperienced.'

Her eyes darkened. 'It was wonderful,' she said in a low, intense voice. 'But surely that has nothing to do with my moral sense.'

'Blackmail is a particularly abhorrent crime, and I

couldn't reconcile someone who'd perpetrated that with the woman who'd unravelled so completely in my arms. When we made love there was no pretence, no fake shyness—you were utterly mine. Without holding anything back you gave me yourself openly and wholeheartedly.'

'Yes,' she said dreamily, because she could say it now.

In an ironic voice he said, 'Not that I admitted it to myself. It took me quite a while to accept that this feeling of intense rightness—I can't describe it any other way— was honest and valid. I even enjoyed quarrelling with you, and for the first time I had some inkling of why my parents stayed together.'

'I'm not normally quarrelsome,' she said, adding with a sigh, 'Only when you're being particularly obnoxious. And I was hurt—I wanted so much for you to believe me, to know that I simply didn't have it in me to blackmail anyone. It really hurt when everyone believed I'd done it, especially to Miss Popham because she'd been so good to me—she wasn't soft or openly affectionate, but she always had time for me. I suppose you could say she gave me all the mothering I ever had.'

'Then in that case I suggest we go down and see her before we get married.' He kissed her startled mouth with tenderness, then lifted his head and surveyed her. 'I wish I could replace those unhappy memories. But for what it's worth, it wasn't just the sex—in fact, I hadn't known you for long before I realised that the so-called evidence could be read two ways. Oh, I fought it—until a few days ago I fought it—I even tried to exorcise how I felt by asking you to be my mistress. But in my heart I knew I was a goner— that I'd never be free of you again.'

He adjusted his grip so that her head fell back onto his shoulder and he could look into her face. It was too soon to be able to enjoy her feelings; she felt oddly fragile, but it was wonderful to be able to return his tender survey with her heart in her eyes.

A boundless upwelling of love and gratitude calmed her. Kain seemed to understand; he didn't attempt to do anything more than hold her as though she was the most precious burden in the world. Later, she knew dreamily, they would make love and it would be flash and fire and drama, but in these moments of silent communion she sensed they were forging something wonderful and lasting.

He said, 'When that woman from your home town told me—as a friend, of course—that you were a thoroughly bad lot, I knew then that I didn't believe a word of it.'

'I saw her telling you.' Sable looked back with pity on herself that night.

'She really enjoyed that,' he said with a cold, icy inflection that made her shiver, 'until I warned her if she wanted to face a lawsuit for defamation of character she was going the right way about it.'

'So that's why—' Sable stopped.

'What?' he asked dangerously. And when she didn't answer he tilted her face so that he could read her expression. 'Tell me.'

Sable shrugged. 'She just muttered that we deserved each other.'

The danger faded from his face. 'I certainly don't deserve you,' he said and kissed her again, breaking it off to carefully deposit her further away on the sofa, saying in a thickened voice that sent erotic little shivers down her spine, 'I love you so much.'

'So why am I sitting alone?'

His smile faded. 'Because I want you right now, and I know you're tired and you need food.' He added with a chilling certainty, 'The moment I heard Frensham's voice I knew I wouldn't trust him with anything, much less the truth. He'll never bother you again, and he certainly won't go spreading any more lies.'

As though he couldn't help himself he touched her mouth, her eyes, the glossy silk of her hair. 'All the time we've been together every word, every action, has shown me how honest you are. I don't care what Miss Popham has to say—you're the proof of your own innocence.'

He paused, then added grimly, 'If you like, you can point out that blackmailing you puts me in the same class as Frensham.'

'Don't be an idiot,' she told him lovingly, closing his lips with her hand.

He looked down at her, his mouth tender. 'You're letting me off far too easily. While I've been keeping my head firmly buried in the sand, you've had a rotten time.'

She shook her head, giving him a shy smile. 'No, not all the time.'

'The only extenuation I can plead is that I wasn't enjoying myself either—and when I realised that I was actually falling in love with you it made me savage and stupid.'

'It doesn't matter,' she said swiftly. She smiled at him, luxuriating in the delight of being able to show her love openly. 'But we'll never get in such a tangle again, will we.'

'No. And I don't deserve to be so freely forgiven, either, but I have to admit I'm glad.' He kissed her then, properly, and when she was weak and clinging to him, he murmured, 'When are you going to marry me?'

Shaken, giddily reckless with love and hope, she felt forced to point out, 'We've only known each other for a few weeks. Are you absolutely sure?'

He held her gaze. 'Absolutely,' he said, so intensely the

words held all the force of a vow. 'Only you. For the rest of my life.'

In the eyes she'd once thought so cold, so emotionless, Sable read her future—a love that would never die. Her heart swelled with a passionate, unwavering adoration. She fought back another spurt of tears and whispered, 'Only you for ever and ever.'

His head came down to hers, and this kiss blotted out the past with the promise of a shining, rapturous life together.

* * * * *

*Harlequin Presents® is thrilled to introduce
a sexy new duet,*
HOT BED OF SCANDAL, *by Kelly Hunter!*
Read on for a sneak peek of the first book
EXPOSED: MISBEHAVING WITH THE MAGNATE.

'I'M ATTRACTED to you and don't see why I should deny it. Our kiss in the garden suggests you're not exactly indifferent to me. The solution seems fairly straightforward.'

'You want me to become the comte's convenient mistress?'

'I'm not a comte,' Luc said. 'All I have is the castle.'

'All right, the billionaire's preferred plaything, then.'

'I'm not a billionaire, either. Yet.' His lazy smile warned her it was on his to-do list. 'No, I want you to become my outrageously beautiful, independently wealthy lover.'

'Isn't that the same option?'

'No, you might have noticed that the wording's a little different.'

'They're just words, Luc. The outcome's the same.'

'It's an attitude thing.' He looked at her, his smile crookedly charming. 'So what do you say?'

To an affair with the likes of Luc Duvalier? 'I say it's dangerous. For both of us.'

Luc's eyes gleamed. 'There is that.'

'Not to mention insane.'

'Quite possibly. Was that a yes?'

Gabrielle really didn't know what to say. 'So how do we start this thing? If I were to agree to it. Which I haven't.' Yet.

'We start with dinner. Tonight. No expectations beyond a pleasant evening with fine food, fine wine and good company. And we see what happens.'

'I don't know,' she said, reaching for her coffee. 'It seems a little…'

'Straightforward?' he suggested. 'Civilized?'

'For us, yes,' she murmured. 'Where would we eat? Somewhere public or in private?'

'Somewhere public,' he said firmly. 'The restaurant I'm thinking of is a fine one—excellent food, small premises and always busy. A man might take his lover there if he was trying to keep his hands off her.'

'Would I meet you there?' she said.

'I will, of course, collect you,' he said, playing the autocrat and playing it well. 'Shall I meet you there,' he murmured in disbelief. 'What kind of question is that?'

'Says the new generation Frenchman,' she countered. 'Liberated, egalitarian, nonsexist…'

'Helpful, attentive, chivalrous…' he added with a reckless smile. 'And very beddable.'

He was that.

'All right,' she said. 'I'll give you the day—and tonight—to prove that a civilized, pleasurable and manageable affair wouldn't be beyond us. If you can prove this to my satisfaction, I'll make love with you. If this gets out of hand, however…'

'Yes?' he said silkily. 'What do you suggest?'

Gabrielle leaned forward, elbows on the table. Luc leaned forward, too. 'Well, I don't know about you,' she murmured, 'but I'm a clever, outrageously beautiful, independently wealthy woman. I plan to run.'

*This sparky story is full of passion, wit and scandal
and will leave you wanting more!
Look for*
EXPOSED: MISBEHAVING WITH THE MAGNATE
Available March 2010

HARLEQUIN *Presents*

*Two families torn apart by secrets and desire
are about to be reunited in*

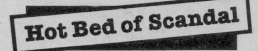

Hot Bed of Scandal

a sexy new duet by

Kelly Hunter

EXPOSED: MISBEHAVING WITH THE MAGNATE

#2905 Available March 2010

Gabriella Alexander returns to the French vineyard she
was banished from after being caught in flagrante with the
owner's son Lucien Duvalier—only to finish what they started!

REVEALED: A PRINCE AND A PREGNANCY

#2913 Available April 2010

Simone Duvalier wants Rafael Alexander and always has, but
they both get more than they bargained for when a night of
passion and a royal revelation rock their world!

THE WESTMORELANDS

NEW YORK TIMES
bestselling author

BRENDA JACKSON

HOT WESTMORELAND NIGHTS

Ramsey Westmoreland knew better than to lust after the hired help. But Chloe, the new cook, was just so delectable. Though their affair was growing steamier, Chloe's motives became suspicious. And when he learned Chloe was carrying his child this Westmoreland Rancher had to choose between pride or duty.

Available March 2010 wherever books are sold.

Always Powerful, Passionate and Provocative.

**Presents Extra brings you
two new exciting collections!**

WEDLOCKED!

*Marriages made in haste…
and love comes later*

The Konstantos Marriage Demand #93
by KATE WALKER

Claiming his Wedding Night #94
by LEE WILKINSON

THE ITALIAN'S BABY

Pleasured, pregnant and at the Italian's mercy!

The Italian's Ruthless Baby Bargain #95
by MARGARET MAYO

Pregnant with the De Rossi Heir #96
by MAGGIE COX

*Available March 2010
from Harlequin Presents EXTRA!*

HPEMAR10

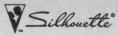

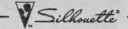

SPECIAL EDITION

FROM *USA TODAY* BESTSELLING AUTHOR

CHRISTINE RIMMER

A BRIDE FOR JERICHO BRAVO

Marnie Jones had long ago buried her wild-child impulses and opted to be "safe," romantically speaking. But one look at born rebel Jericho Bravo and she began to wonder if her thrill-seeking side was about to be revived. Because if ever there was a man worth taking a chance on, there he was, right within her grasp....

Available in March
wherever books are sold.

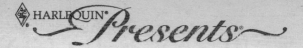

Coming Next Month
Available February 23, 2010

#2899 MARCHESE'S FORGOTTEN BRIDE Michelle Reid

#2900 GREEK TYCOON, INEXPERIENCED MISTRESS Lynne Graham
Pregnant Brides

#2901 THE SHEIKH'S IMPATIENT VIRGIN Kim Lawrence

#2902 BOUGHT: DESTITUTE YET DEFIANT Sarah Morgan
Self-Made Millionaires

#2903 THE INNOCENT'S SURRENDER Sara Craven

#2904 HIS MISTRESS FOR A MILLION Trish Morey

**#2905 EXPOSED: MISBEHAVING WITH THE MAGNATE
Kelly Hunter**
Hot Bed of Scandal

#2906 PUBLIC AFFAIR, SECRETLY EXPECTING Heidi Rice